THE PRICE OF EVIL

By   Brian Wright

THE PRICE OF EVIL
CONTENTS
CHAPTERS

This is the real England thought Trevor Nightingale as he sat at his table in the private bar of the Six Bells and looked out across the village green. The green itself was about half an acre of grassland with a cricket pitch cordoned off in its centre, round its edges were lime trees and the other side of them was a roadway that ran right round the green. At the edges of the green he could see the cricket pavilion, a small playground and the war memorial. Beyond the road were houses, the parish church and the few remaining shops as well as the Six Bells. Upper Burford was situated in a valley of the South Downs with the hills on the two sides and at the far end of the village. It was at the end of the road that led from the main east west route across West Sussex and, in some ways, its location had been its protection because the road into the village did not lead anywhere. From the top of the green there was simply a narrow lane that climbed up towards the Downs and then came to an abrupt end. Between the village and the main road, the land was flatter and it was there that the old Manor House had been located. Difficulty in obtaining staff and death duties had led to it being sold and it was now the headquarters for a large financial group. In some ways this had proved a salvation for the village as the arrival of its personnel had caused the building of some new houses and the increase in families meant the number of children attending the village school had ensured its survival. In addition the stables at the Six Bells had been converted into a kitchen and dining room and had earned a well deserved reputation that brought quite a lot of visitors and money into the village.

Trevor completed his survey of the green and its surroundings and his attention returned to the war memorial. He was a landscape gardener by profession and had won gold medals at all the major flower shows. It was hardly surprising therefore that the Parish Council had turned to him when they decided, at long last, to do something about the area surrounding the war memorial. He took a notebook from his pocket, adjusted his propelling pencil and began to make some sketches of possible ways in which the site could be improved.

'Designing a new garden Mr Nightingale 'Norman Alkham the landlord of the Six Bells asked as he brought over a refill of Trevor's half pint of lager.
'Not exactly Norman, I have been asked by the Parish Council to see what I can do with the area round the war memorial'
'Its coming up election time so I suppose they feel they ought to have something to show for their time in office.'

Shortly after the bar opened with a flourish to admit two women. If anyone had been drinking to excess, they may well have thought they were seeing double but, in fact, the new arrivals were Olivia and Olga Sanderson who were identical twins who always dressed in matching clothes to add confusion to identification. Both had had very successful careers in the entertainment industry. Olivia, the elder by five minutes, had been a vocalist with big bands and on the stage, radio and television. Originally christened Janet Sanderson she had adopted the stage name of Olivia. Her sister, christened Sylvia, had been a ballet dancer and assumed the stage name of Olga Sandova and been principal ballerina in a number of international ballet companies. Each had married wealthy businessmen who had had the good manners to die reasonably young and leave their widows with more than adequate finances. At which point they had decided to share a home and had moved to the village. Today they were dressed in washed out blue denim suits with red shirts and yachting hats. Those in the know realised that the art in identifying who was who was that while both wore ruby rings Olivia wore hers on her right hand and Olga on her left.

'Two of the usual please Norman' called Olga, the first one over the threshold.
'Busy as usual darling' Olivia said to Trevor as they slipped into seats at his table. 'Another master stroke for the Chelsea?'
'No, just some thoughts on the new garden for the war memorial'
'Don't tell me the council are actually going to spend some money.'
'Actually, I think the local British Legion are footing half the cost.'
'Typical' snorted Olga 'the BL put up the funds and that useless crowd take all the credit.'
'If you don't like them darling' said Olivia' why don't you stand for the Council yourself?'
'Very funny! There would be murder done at the first meeting if I got elected.'
'I thought that Donald might be here for an aperitif'
'I haven't seen him today' said Trevor.
'Hang on I thought I saw his Man Friday in the saloon. Norman,' she called, 'if Mr Whitehouse is in the bar could you ask him whether his lord and master will be coming in today?'
'I say 'Olivia said 'have you heard what that ghastly man Burgess told Verity Trumper?'
'What has been up to now?' asked Trevor.
'He stopped that great car of his outside the shop and wound down his window when he saw Verity passing. He told her that he thought she ought to know as Chair of the Burford Hall and Green Committee that he planned to organise a pop concert on the green. You know the sort of thing an enormous stage and speakers that would break your ear drums at three hundred yards.'
'Did he say why he wanted to do that?'
'He said it would put the village on the map. But, of course, it is a publicity stunt for his business. He was going to call it the Burford Bonanza. Anyway, the Green was going to be covered with burger stalls and bars as well as hordes of

people. He said he could arrange parking and camping in the fields between the village and the main road'
'Doesn't he need approval for something like that? 'asked Trevor
'Possibly but by the time he has greased enough palms, I reckon he has half the District Council in his pocket, he will probably be given the green light.'
'What did Verity say? I can't imagine she was impressed with the idea.'
'I gather she told him that the village would fight such an idea tooth and nail'
'The next meeting of the Hall and Green Committee is going to be interesting.'

The man they were talking about was Nigel Burgess who was principal partner in the chain of estate agents called Burgess Homes as well as the owner of various property owning and development companies. He had bought an old barn at the end of the lane leading from the village and turned it into the most luxurious house in the village. He had assumed that ownership of the biggest and most expensive house carried with it the lordship of the manor or something similar and he was not best pleased when the existing inhabitants declined to touch their forelocks to him. In the short time he had lived in the village he had succeeded in rubbing up the wrong way practically every one of the more affluent residents. He gave loud parties to his friends who arrived in large and expensive cars and caused traffic hazards to other residents as well as creating disturbances when they left the village in the small hours. He thought he had prior right to the best tables in the Six Bells dining room whenever he wanted them and demanded the church bells be silenced because they woke him too early on Sunday morning.

The door to the Saloon bar admitted a man in his late fifties dressed in a dark grey suit, a white shirt and a discreet tie. He was Harold Whitehouse.
'Harold 'said Olivia 'do you know where your lord and master is?
'He received an early call from the Rector asking him to visit Mrs Welton who it seems was terminally ill.'
'Margaret Welton 'exclaimed Olga 'the poor dear. She must be nearly one hundred and three.'
'I understand, 'Harold replied gravely 'that her one hundred and third birthday is due in about three weeks.'
'Why didn't Lionel Trumper go to see her she is far and away his oldest parishioner 'Olga said.
'I understand the Rector had an important meeting to address at Southampton University. He considered it important to get his message across to the audience.'
'Was he speaking to the Student Union or something?' asked Trevor.
'No, sir, he was addressing a conference on the history of the role of the Chorus in Greek Theatre.'

'That man is impossible 'snorted Olivia 'here was his oldest parishioner dying and he goes off to talk to a group of fusty academics about ancient Greek theatre.'
'I saw the undertaker's vehicle pass by a short while ago' said Harold, 'so I presume his lordship will be with you shortly'

He had no sooner retired to the Saloon Bar than the door to the Private Bar opened to admit a tall man with steel grey hair wearing a dark blue blazer, black trousers and a clerical collar. He was Donald Craigton the third Baron Acaster who was the curate at the church of St Michael and All Angels, Upper Burford. To the village he was known as the Reverend Craigton and to his friends as Donald. He did nothing to flaunt his title.

'Ah, Donald, there you are darling' said Olga, what news of poor Margaret Welton?'
'She passed away at about 9.45 this morning. It was very peaceful. One minute she was with us and the next she had gone to the God she had served so faithfully for so many years.'
'A beautiful way to go' murmured Olivia.
'I must admit that one can but hope to go the same way' added Trevor.

Norman brought through a dry sherry for the curate.

'Had she any family? Olga asked.
'I don't think so. She had out survived all of them. I am going into Chichester this afternoon to register the death and to see Taskers her solicitors.'
'You are a Good Samaritan, Donald' Olga patted his arm.
'We had been talking about the latest Burgess plan for the village' Trevor said trying to lighten the mood.
'Yes', added Olivia 'the pop concert on the green'
'That is not his latest idea 'Donald grinned.
'Heaven protect us' sighed Olga 'what's he up to now?'
'I heard from Lionel Trumper, who got it from Verity, who got it from one of the District councillors that he wants to buy Verney's Copse '
'What on earth for? It's nothing but trees and shrubs. He could never build houses up there.'
'No; he wants to use at as what he calls a recreation area.'
'What kind of recreation?' asked Trevor.
'Apparently it is to be for off-road four-wheel vehicles and paint ball shooting'
'Heaven protect us' shrieked Olga 'he can't do that can he?'
'What worries me is that he has quite a number of the councillors in his pocket' Trevor pointed out.
'Then the village will have to stop him 'said Olga

'If that man isn't careful, 'said Olivia through gritted teeth 'someone is going to do something drastic.'

Alison Oakes shook hands with the two men who had come to see her off and climbed into her Jaguar sports car, waived her hand and set off from Canterbury back to West Sussex. She was feeling elated because her day had been marked with success. Her company had secured the appointment as public relations consultants to The Magpie Brewery Company which was one of the largest of such organisations in the south of England. Not only that but she had been told that her friend Nigel Burgess would receive, in the next two days, official confirmation that his firm Burgess Property Management had won the contract to be property consultants to the brewery. It was a double strike. Yet there was an element of irony in all this.

Alison and Nigel had first met the chairman of the brewery at a business development convention in London. That original contact had led to an invitation to bid for the business of the brewery in their individual areas of expertise. Alison, after having worked for a number of years for one of the major international public relations firms had decided to branch out on her own and to bring her own personal approach to public relations consultancy. The gamble she had taken had paid off and she now owned a small but highly rated and profitable agency with some blue-chip names among her clients. Nigel, who had started his business life as a sales representative for a firm of estate agents in Croydon and Brighton had moved on to set up his own agency in Chichester. This had grown till it was represented in every large Sussex town; not only that but he had set up and ran a number of companies that dealt with property management and letting and property development with the result that he was now an extremely wealthy man. When they had met at a dinner at a livery company in London Alison had found Nigel an interesting and pleasant companion. Their friendship had developed until Alison had moved into Nigel's new house on the edge of the South Downs. It was a big and luxurious barn conversion with landscaped gardens and beautiful views over the adjacent Down land. Theirs had never been a great romance and Alison, a pragmatist, knew it could not last. Nigel was not monogamous by nature and, sure enough, after some months his attentions switched to someone else. The result was that they agreed that, once the negotiations with The Magpie Brewery were complete, she would move out to make way for his latest conquest. They delayed this move while the negotiations were proceeding because, initially, they had given Magpie to understand that they were a couple. Now that the contracts were secured there would be few if any occasions that their individual organisations would be involved in the same project. Thus, it was that Alison, in preparation for her move, had bought a small house in Itchenor which was convenient for commuting to her business premises in Chichester.

She stopped about half way home to get some petrol and took the opportunity to ring Nigel with the news. There was no reply either from his office number or from the house. Damn the man, she thought when she was back on the road it was agreed that I would phone him with what had happened today. If he was too busy practicing horizontal gymnastics with that damned blonde, she would not only give him a piece of her mind but would have to control herself from giving him a slap round the ear. As it was it was after seven fifteen when her car pulled into the driveway at The Great Barn. Nigel's top of the range Mercedes was already in its parking place outside the double garage. Getting out of her car and stretching herself after her journey she picked up her briefcase and entered the house through the front door. She called out that she was back but there was no response. Where was the man? She crossed the big lounge and went into the kitchen. He wasn't there either but he had been because there was evidence that he had made himself a coffee. The back door was ajar and she went outside and called his name. Once again there was no reply. She moved round the side of the house on to the patio and there, at a table, was Nigel. He was slumped over a newspaper.

'Nigel' she called thinking he must have fallen asleep but he did not seem to hear her.
She crossed to the table and shook him by the shoulder. He still did not move and she put her hand on his back and shook him harder. It was then that she felt something on her hand and looking at her palm saw a bright red stain. Her eyes looked down at his back and she could see a small hole just under his shoulder blade which was surrounded by blood. For a moment she stood stock still and had to fight off a wave of nausea. Then she staggered back into the house and dialled 999.

Inspector Albert Love from the police station in Chichester watched as a dapper man in dinner jacket and black trousers knelt over the body that had been photographed in situ and was now laying on the patio. He was Dr Oscar Penrose the police surgeon.
'What can you tell me doctor? 'Love asked.
'He's dead 'the doctor who disliked the Inspector intensely replied, ' and don't ask stupid questions Love'
'I mean how did he die and when?'
'He died from a single stab wound from a narrow-bladed knife that entered straight into the left ventricle. As to when I would suggest within the last hour but I will be able to be more positive when I have him properly prepared for autopsy. You can move him now when you want.'
'You'll let me have your report tomorrow doctor?'
'You will get it when its ready.'
The doctor got to his feet and made to leave.

'Next time you find a body Love kindly do not do so just as I am about to take my wife out to dinner.'
For all the effect it had on the Inspector he may as well have saved his breath.
'Sparrow' Love called to his sergeant, 'what have you found?'
'Nothing of any interest sir. As you know the back door was open when we arrived and Miss Oakes says it was like that when she returned home. The deceased would have opened the front door when he arrived and seems to have paused in the kitchen to make a coffee and then to come out here. Whoever stuck a knife in him must have come round the side of the house but if he kept to the made-up footpaths and the patio there will be no footprints. SOCO are looking for finger prints inside the house and will process out here when the body is removed. I have sent some men into the village to see if we can confirm the time that he passed through on his way home. Given the sort of car he drove that may be easier than if it was a more run of the mill model. They are to do the same for Miss Oakes car.
'What other access is there to the garden?'
'There is just the driveway from the road which leads to a side gate which is locked. There are hedges all around the rear garden with two gateways, one of which leads into a lane that goes up on to the downs and the other into a copse. We are still checking where that leads to. It looks as if someone got in by one of those entrances and possibly waited for the deceased and pounced before he knew what was happening. The doctor said that death was practically instantaneous.'
'Get the body removed Sparrow. Let me know if you find anything especially the knife. I am going to talk to the woman who claims to have found him.'

Once through the kitchen, which was luxurious enough Love entered a large lounge which was furnished with quality items and tasteful décor and lighting. A young woman was sitting in an armchair and on a table before her was a glass which still had some whisky or brandy in it. A woman PC stood in the doorway leading to the front door and Love indicated to her to stay in place. He produced his identity details and showed them to the young woman.

'You are Miss Alison Oakes I believe '
'That is correct'
'Can you tell me how you came to find Mr Burgess?'
'I live here and was returning from having been in Canterbury on business all day.'
'When did you last see Mr Burgess?'
'About eight thirty this morning when I left to drive to Canterbury.'
'You arrived here at what time?'

'I am not sure of the exact time but it was about three or four minutes before I called 999. I simply parked the car, entered the house, dropped my bag and my briefcase, went through the kitchen into the garden and there he was.'
'What time did you leave Canterbury?'
'About five o'clock. The people I was visiting can confirm that.'
'Who was that?'
'The Magpie Brewery Company. I was at their headquarters from ten thirty this morning until five this afternoon.'
'This was a business call?'
'It was. I had better explain. I run a small but successful public relations company and had been tendering to be appointed consultants to the Brewery Group.'
'You didn't see or speak to Mr Burgess all day?'
'No. I tried to phone him at about six fifteen this evening but there was no reply either for here or for his office number.'
'Where did you make this call?'
'From a pub near Lewes where I called in to have a soft drink.'
'Do you remember the name of the pub?'
'Yes, it was the Sussex Yeoman.'
'Do you know of anyone who might wish to harm Mr Burgess?'
'I don't. He was a very successful businessman. I suppose that in building that success he might have offended someone or other but I have no idea whom.'
'Did you have a business relationship with Mr Burgess' firm?'
'I did. My company acted as public relations consultants for his group of companies.'
'He had more than one company?'
'He had a number of business interests which necessitated a number of independent companies.
'May I ask what your personal relationship with Mr Burgess was?'
'I have lived here for six months. We were close friends.'
'Does that mean you were lovers Miss Oakes?'
'We did not always behave as if were in a monastery or nunnery but I would not describe our relationship as being akin to a marriage. It was an arrangement suited us both at the time.'
'At the time?' Love seemed to pounce on the phrase.'
'It was never intended to be permanent. In fact, we agreed that I should move out of this house and, to that end, I have bought a cottage in Itchenor I am due to leave here tomorrow morning.'
'I regret that will not be possible.'
'What do you mean? You surely don't suspect me of killing Nigel, do you?'
'It is not a question of suspecting anyone Miss Oakes but this property has now become a crime scene. Officers will have to carry out a thorough search of the house and grounds. This means that your goods must remain here until I am

able to agree to their release. Also, I wish you, please to stay here until the inquest is held.'

'But I have a business to run. We have our head office in East Pallant in Chichester. I need to be there.'

'I am afraid that for a couple of days you will have to organise your business from here. I may then be able to agree to your returning to work.'

'This is ridiculous' Alison shouted 'You make me sound like a criminal.'

'As the officer in charge of this investigation I am taking routine steps necessary to allow us to do our work.'

With this Inspector Love walked back through the kitchen and into the garden.

'Sergeant Sparrow, 'he called.

When his sergeant appeared, he asked.

'Found anything useful?'

'A lad in the village saw the deceased's car come through at about six forty. Nothing as yet about the young lady's car.'

'Have you found the weapon?'

'No sir. We are extending the search into the copse and along the lane. Have you had any luck sir?'

'I think I know who killed him.'

'Who is that sir?'

'That young woman.'

'But she says she did not leave Canterbury until five this evening and did not get her until just before she called 999'

'That is what she says. But is it true? I want her leave time checked and I want to know how long it takes to drive from Canterbury to here. Oh, and I want enquiries made at a pub called The Sussex Yeoman near Lewes to see if they recall her making a phone call from there and if so at what time. If they do then find out how long it takes to get from there to here.'

'What makes you think she did it sir ?'

'It's not unknown sergeant for the person who finds the body to actually have killed the victim' Love said sarcastically. 'Added to the fact that she had fallen out with the deceased and he had thrown her out, even if she says they were parting amicably. She has to be the prime suspect. Our job is to prove she did it.'

Back in the house Alison refilled her glass and sat down again. Then she suddenly put her head into her arms and started to cry.

CHAPTER 3

The following morning Inspector Love was in his office early and, having disposed of some routine paper work, he was reading through the various reports that had come in overnight.

'Good morning sir ' said Sergeant Sparrow entering with some more reports.
'Anything new to report Sparrow?'
'No sir, nothing of particular interest. Still no sign of the weapon, it begins to look as though the perpetrator took it with them.'
'Have we finished with the house yet ?'
'Not yet sir, it's a big place and we are taking it apart carefully.'
'What about the travel times claimed by the Oakes female ?'
'Traffic are working on that but will want to do a run at the same time of day before giving an opinion.'
'Ask the police along the route if any of them saw the car, after all it's not your average vehicle, and if so where and at what time.'
'That's in hand sir.'
'Although I am quite sure it was the young woman who did it we can't forget other lines of investigation. I don't want some smart arsed counsel claiming the police had closed minds on the case from day one. Burgess was a businessman and a successful one by all accounts so we need to know all there is to know about him, his business interests and his friends and enemies. Get on to Finance section at HQ and ask for someone to help with the business side of the investigation.'
'Actually sir, we have just had a chap assigned to us on a temporary basis as part of the fast track training programme. I gather that before he joined the force, he was a qualified accountant with one of the big firms in London. I was wondering if might not be a good idea to use him.'
'Fast track training programmes' snorted Love' when will they learn there is no substitute to experience. Alright, go ahead and use this man. Tell him we want to know all about Burgess and his business, warts and all.'
'Yes sir.'
'Now I am going to Upper Burford to see what I can pick up by way of local information about the deceased and his lady friend. Get in touch with Penrose and find out as much as you can about the sort of weapon that was used. It's all very well saying it was a knife but I want to know what kind of knife it was. Go through the autopsy report when it comes and give me a précis.'

When he got to the village Love sought out the local constable and questioned him on what he knew about Burgess and to get a clearer picture of the village hierarchy.

'There's no denying he was not popular with some of the people' said
Constable Peter Watson.
'Who and why ?' demanded Love.
'Mainly the people who have kind of run the village for years. He came here as
the owner of the biggest and most expensive house in the place which he
seemed to think made him the modern equivalent of the squire. From what I
hear he wasn't exactly diplomatic in the way the acted with the long-term
residents. Seems to have put up the backs of most of them one way or another. '
'What about you? 'asked Love 'did you have any contact with him ?'
'Not much' said Watson 'I had to ask him to move that great car of his on one
occasion which didn't go down too well but he did as he was asked eventually.'
'Who are the people whose noses you think he put out of joint ?'
Watson gave him some names and pointed out where they lived.

Love's first port of call was at a large house in one corner of the green. The
door was opened by a man in his fifties dressed in corduroy trousers and a
check shirt. Love produced his identity and asked if he could speak to him.
Trevor Nightingale showed him into a lounge with a large picture window that
looked out on to a big garden that seemed to be divided into a number of
different plots.

'I am investigating the death of Mr Nigel Burgess.'
'So, it's true is it? 'Trevor asked 'I heard a rumour about something happening
at that big house.'
'You knew Mr Burgess?'
'Yes, I knew him but I would not say that we were close.'
'Can you think of anyone who might have wished him harm?'
'That's an interesting question 'grinned Trevor 'it's no secret he was not the
most popular man in the village. But I can't think of anyone who would resort
to physical violence against him.'
'Why do you say he was unpopular Mr Nightingale?'
'I don't know how much you know about village life Inspector. Upper Burford
is in some ways somewhat old fashioned, many of its inhabitants have lived
here for a long time. There is still not exactly a village squirearchy but an
accepted way in which village affairs are organised. Burgess, a man of means,
builds himself a big house and thinks this means he is top man in the village. He
wasn't. If he wanted to occupy that role, he would have had to earn it but he
didn't. He just charged in and thought that everyone would kowtow to what he
said and he soon found out that they did not. The result was that he fell out with
nearly everyone he came into contact with. '
'Does that include you sir ?'
'As a matter of fact, it does. I may as well tell you the story before you get some
garbled version. I am a landscape gardener by profession and, even if I say so

myself, I have been reasonably successful. When he came here Burgess asked
me to design and install the garden at his house. He was a difficult client from
day one but I managed to get the job done and I think it was a success. When I
submitted my account, he suggested that I waived the charge on the grounds
that he would be able to put more business my way. I told him I would see him
court and he paid up. Since then we have not spoken.'
'I see. As a matter of interest sir, can you tell me where you were between say
six and seven thirty last evening?'
'Am I a suspect? 'Trevor laughed.
'Not at all but I am trying to fill in a picture of what was happening in the
village at that time.'
'I am not married and I live alone. I was working at my desk all afternoon and,
after listening to the early evening news, I had a shower, changed and went
down to the Six Bells for a meal. I left here about seven thirty and had booked a
table for seven forty-five. They should be able to confirm when I arrived.'
'I see sir, 'said Love 'so in fact you have no alibi for the time I mentioned. '
It seems not. Is that important?'
'I am unable to say at the moment'

 I wouldn't put my shirt on that man solving the Daily Mail children's
crossword let alone a murder said Trevor as he watched the Inspector go down
his driveway.

Love's next call was at a large bungalow with a carefully tended front garden
and a path up to a black painted front door. He rang the bell expecting it to be
answered by a white-haired lady dressed in a twin set and tweed skirt and
wearing a pearl necklace. In fact, your typical village spinster of a certain age.
To his surprise the door was opened by someone of medium height with fair
hair and with a carefully made up face. She was wearing denim trousers, a white
shirt with a bright blue scarf at her neck. On her feet she wore high heeled blue
sandals.
'Can I help you?' she smiled
Love produced his identity.'
'I was hoping to speak to Miss Sanderson.'
'Then your hope has been met, I am Olivia Sanderson'
'I am investigating the circumstances surrounding the death of Mr Nigel
Burgess. Could I you spare me a moment or two'
'I had heard that Burgess had died but I didn't know it involved a police
investigation. You had better come in.'
She led him across a brightly decorated hallway into what appeared to be a
study the walls of which were covered in photographs that all appeared to be of
either a ballet dancer or a singer.
'Shades of a past life', she laughed seeing his eyes take in the photos. 'I am the

singer and my sister was the dancer. Talking of her I had better go and find her.'
She had only been gone for a minute or so before the door opened and she re-appeared.
'Good morning ' she said ' I don't think we have met.'
Love was taken back. How could she forget. He had introduced himself only minutes ago. Was she suffering senile dementia, Before he could say anything the door opened again and, to Love's amazement there was a second
woman who not only looked like the first but was dressed in exactly the same way.'
'There you are darling' said the new arrival ' have you introduced yourself to the Inspector? No, this is my sister Inspector, she is Olga Sanderson who was known as Olga Barisova when she was dancing. Please do sit down.'
Gathering his wits and looking again at these two women who were as like as peas in a pod and about as far away from his idea of village spinsters as it was possible to get.
 Love spoke. 'As I mentioned to Miss Olivia I am the police officer leading the enquiry into the death of Mr Nigel Burgess. I believe you ladies knew him.'
'We had met him' replied Olga 'but that was all.'
'In these cases, 'said Love ponderously, 'it is necessary to speak to all those who knew the deceased. Doing so helps us to get a clearer picture of him '
'I don't think we can add a great deal to what you already will have learned' said Olivia. 'We were not exactly friends with him.'
'But you know the village well?'
'Of course, we have lived here for a number of years.'
'Can you think of anyone who might wish to harm Mr Burgess?'
'I don't think it's a secret' replied Olga' that he was not the most popular man in the village.'
'Why was that Miss Sanderson,'
'He had an unfortunate manner. He seemed to think that as he owned The Great Barn he should be seen as sort of local squire, ignoring the fact that he was a newcomer.'
'That kind of thing does not go down well in a village like this 'added Olivia.
'Were there any serious quarrels?' asked Love.
'Not serious quarrels. It was more that he annoyed people by his behaviour. On occasions, he could be very rude about other residents.'
'Can you give me any examples?'
'My sister', said Olivia 'runs a small ballet class for little girls in the village. One evening we called in at the Six Bells where Mr Burgess was drinking with some of his friends. On seeing us he said something to his group which caused them considerable amusement. Someone who overheard what he had said told another friend of ours that it was to the effect that Olga was supposed to be a so called ballet dancer. Looking at the way she walked she looked more like a

constipated goose than a dying swan. '

'He also said, 'added Olga 'that Olivia had been, a so called singer, the sort that used to appear on a Saturday night at the Ritz Ballroom in Bognor Regis whereas, in fact, she had sung with all the leading bands and appeared on both radio and television.'

'Not the sort of comments to endear himself to one.'

'But not the sort,' added Olivia quickly 'to drive either of us to murder. As professional artistes we had become inured to criticism.'

'Part of a police investigation is tracking the movements of people during the critical period. Could you please tell me where you were last evening between six and seven thirty?'

'I hope you are not suggesting we are suspects 'Olga said in a cold voice.

'It is only by knowing where everyone was at the time in question, we can obtain a clear picture Miss Sanderson. Where were you for example?'

'After we had eaten our tea, I came into this room to write some letters and was here until nearly eight o'clock.'

'And I was in the kitchen making some bread 'added Olivia.

'Were you in any sort of contact during that time either with each other or with someone from outside? Love enquired.

'No' they replied in unison.

'So it would be right to say that neither of you has an alibi.'

'I can show you the bread I made, although we ate some for breakfast.'

'That does not prove that you baked it yesterday evening.'

'I can't prove I wrote those letters then either. In any event I walked to the post just after eight so no longer have them.'

'Did either of you see or hear anything unusual during the time in question or last evening at any time ?'

'No' they replied in unison.

'Does that make us suspects ? demanded Olivia.

'At the moment madam no-one is a suspect and no-one is not a suspect.'

'That man is the limit' said Olivia when she had shown the Inspector out. 'If he talks to everyone else like that I can't see the village giving him much help.'

'It's just as well darling that he did not know what you said yesterday morning' laughed Olga.

'What do you mean ?'

'That if Mr Burgess did not take care someone would do something drastic.'

'I must be psychic 'giggled Olivia.

Unimpressed with the people he had questioned so far Inspector Love moved to the next address on his list. It was a large modern house and, on the gate was a sign which read 'The Rectory '. The original rectory had been a much bigger building at the other end of the village that had been built when rectors had large families and numerous servants. The Church Commissioners had sold that property with its large garden and it had been dismantled and replaced by six small mid twentieth century houses. Love rang the bell and the door was answered by a short dark-haired woman wearing a smart two-piece suit with a pale blue jumper and a pearl necklace.

'I would like to speak to the Reverend Trumper' he announced producing his identity.'
'My husband is not at home 'the lady of the house replied crisply 'I do not expect him until this evening. He is a delegate at an important conference in London.'
'You are Mrs Verity Trumper?'
'I am'
'The perhaps I might be able to have a few minutes of your time.'
'In connection with what?'
'I am investigating the death of a Mr Nigel Burgess of this village.'
'And what may I ask makes you think I know anything about that?'
'If I might just come in for a moment, I will explain the reason for my call.'
'Very well, if you insist. Come this way.'
She showed him into the kitchen as if emphasising that he should have called at the back door like any other tradesman. Love took a seat at the table uninvited and opened his notebook.
'I believe that you knew Mr Burgess madam.'
'I had met him, yes.'
'As part of the investigation into the death of anyone the police need to learn all they can about the deceased and this can be assisted by talking to those who knew him.'
'I could not claim to have known him at all well. Our paths had crossed from time to time that is all.'
'Would you say that Mr Burgess was a popular resident ?'
'He may have been with some people but, on the other hand, he may not have been with others.'
'Why do you think he was unpopular with some people madam ?'
'Mr Burgess lived in a big and expensive house; he lived a life of some luxury. That can make people unpopular Inspector.'
'But he fitted into the life of the village satisfactorily?' Love asked as innocently as he could.
'I did not say that. To be quite frank Inspector he did not fit happily into village life. He appeared to think that his house and his money entitled him to be the social leader of the village. He overlooked the fact that this village had existed for many years before he arrived and that it had a well-defined social structure. He had an unfortunate manner which alienated people. For example, he wanted the church bells to be silenced on a Sunday morning as he said it disturbed his rest. This was a ridiculous request. Our church has a fine peal of bells and they

have always been rung to call people to worship, except of course during the war years.'
'Do you know anyone who might have wished to harm him madam ?'
'I do not associate with that type of person Inspector,' said Mrs Trumper haughtily. 'Mr Burgess was at times a nuisance but we have ways and means of dealing with people like that. We have a number of committees and societies, of many of which I am either the president or chair. Those groups are well able to deal with dissident inhabitants without the need to resort to violence. If you want to know who might have harmed the man, I suggest you look at his business and social acquaintances.'
' I have no doubt we shall be doing that madam. Do you have any other specific problems in mind?'
'He stopped me one day in the street and told me he proposed to hold a pop concert on the green. He thought I would like to know as I am the chair of the Village Green Committee. I told him quite clearly that it was most unlikely the committee would give their approval. To which he replied that the views of a load of old fogies didn't cut any ice with him.' The committee was irate at his cheek and refused to countenance the idea. Our secretary wrote and informed him that he would be in breach of the bye laws if he went ahead.'
'What happened ?'
'Nothing. This all happened about two weeks ago.'
'Just one more question, if I may, and that is can you tell me where you were between six o'clock and seven thirty last evening?'
'I trust you are not suggesting that I had anything to do with what happened. If you are, I take the strongest possible objection to such an allegation.'
'This is purely routine madam. Its only by knowing where people were at the significant times that we are able to find out if they heard or saw anything unusual.'
'I was due to attend a meeting of the diocesan committee of the Mothers Union, of which I am the president, which was to be held at the Deanery in Chichester. The meeting was scheduled for eight o'clock. When I had eaten my tea, I collected my papers for the meeting and drove into Chichester.'
'At what time would that be?'
'I left here at about six twenty. I called at The Deanery and had some conversation with the Dean and his wife before the meeting started. The Passmores are long standing friends. In fact, the Dean was a curate to my late father when he was a bishop. I remained to have coffee with the Dean and his wife after the meeting and arrived here at about ten thirty.'
'Was your husband at home during this time madam?'
'My husband was a guest of honour at a symposium at Southampton University and spent the night with the Vice Chancellor who is my cousin.'

'Thank you, madam. If I have understood you correctly you have no-one who is able to corroborate what you say until you arrived in Chichester. In other words, you do not have an alibi.'
'You have my word for it Inspector and that should be sufficient for you or any police officer. Good morning.'

Love quickly found himself back on the pavement. Inside The Rectory Mrs Trumper went to her desk and drawing out paper and pen started to write a letter. The next house on Love's list was another substantial Victorian red brick building with the top half decorated by red tiles. It was the home of a Mr Walter Legg a lawyer with a practice in Chichester. He apparently lived with his sister a Miss Megan Legg. The door was opened by a woman in her early sixties who was dressed in a shapeless jumper and skirt. Her grey hair was cut short and she wore rimless glasses.
'Miss Legg ?'
'Yes ' she answered carefully as if she thought he was an insurance salesman. He produced his identity and, having looked up and down the road she invited him into the house.
'You had better come in here 'she led him into a small room which was full of pieces of material and knitting wool, the walls of which were covered in photos of Girl Guide units.
'How can I be of assistance Inspector,' she asked.
'I am leading the investigation into the death of a Mr Nigel Burgess madam'
'Death 'she exclaimed 'I had no idea. When did he die?'
'Yesterday evening and I regret to have to tell you that his death was neither natural or an accident.'
'Oh dear !'
'Why do you say that madam ?' asked Love
'Because that seems to leave only one alternative. He did not seem to be the man who would take his own life.'
'You knew him ?'
'Not exactly. We had met once or twice and, of course, my brother who is a solicitor acts for him I understand.'
'Did you see or hear anything out of the usual last evening?
'Not that I can remember.'
'Can you think of anyone who might wish him harm ?'
'I am not sure I can answer that question Inspector I hardly knew him and have no idea as to who may have been his enemy.'
'I understand that he had a reputation of being a difficult man. Did you find him that?
'He could be outspoken at times and was not careful who heard what he said. In a village like this such things tend to get repeated back to the person he was talking about.'

'Including yourself madam 'asked Love.
'Well yes, including me. I was a Girl Guide leader for many years and
apparently, he made some disparaging remark about how – how can I put it –
such people as myself always had large posteriors. Also, he would have thought
that people had better things to do than sing camp fire songs and dance round
mushrooms.'
'What was your reaction to that Miss Legg?' he asked trying not to smile.
'I was not very amused Inspector. I was brought up to believe that good
manners cost no-one anything. But of course, he was my brother's client and I
could not enter into an exchange of insults even if I had so wished.'
'One final thing Miss Legg. Can you tell me where you were between six and
seven thirty last evening?'
'Oh dear let me think! Yes, I took my dog Rufus for a short walk up the lane. I
am afraid he thought he saw a rabbit and bolted into the undergrowth. Silly dog,
it took me some minutes to get him back on his lead. We came back here and
then I went into Chichester to a talk at the Assembly Rooms. I left here at about
seven thirty, I was a bit late because of Rufus being so naughty I was a few
minutes late getting to the meeting.'
'You mention a lane Miss Legg. Is that the road leading to Mr Burgess' house?
'Yes, now you come to mention it that is correct. But I didn't get more than
fifty yards up the lane before Rufus ran off and I had to try and get him back.'
'Did you hear any cars or see anyone about ?'
'No Inspector, everything was quiet.'
'So, in fact you have no-one to support your alibi.'
'I suppose not. Is it important?'

Love's last call was at a house called Acaster Lodge. It proved to be detached
house built of oak beams filled with bricks and with mullioned windows and a
heavy oak door. The front gate led up a brick path to the sides of which were
well tended flower borders and a green lawn with attractive herbaceous borders
against the side walls. Love pulled the bell chain and the door was opened by a
middle-aged man dressed in a formal grey suit with a white shirt and quiet tie.
He produced his identity assuming this was probably the curate the Reverend
Donald Craigton.
'Can I be of assistance?' the man asked in quiet voice.
'I should be like to speak to the Reverend Craigton.'
'Please come in Inspector.'
He was led across a wood tiled floor and shown into a small room with a table,
two chairs and some shelves that contained books that appeared to be of a
religious nature.
'Please take a seat.'
The man left and returned a couple of minutes later to open the door and
announce;

'The Reverend Craigton, Inspector.'
Love was surprised by the man who entered. He was expecting that a curate would be a young man but here was a tall slender man with steel grey hair.
'How do you do Inspector 'he held out a hand and gave a firm handshake. 'How can I help?'
Love explained who he was and the purpose of his call.
'A very sad business' said Donald Craigton 'especially in a small and somewhat isolated village such as this.'
'You knew the deceased sir?'
'I had met him, yes, but I would not claim to know him. Perhaps I had better explain. As is my practice with new residents I called to make myself known to Mr Burgess and to offer him any assistance that might be of help to him. He made it quite clear to me that he did not consider my visit welcome. He said he had no religious faith and agreed with Marx that religion was the opiate of the masses. He went on to say that he had no time for the Church of England and all its works. Having delivered himself of that statement he showed me the door. Since then we have not spoken.'
'If you did not know him personally sir what was your impression of him from what you may have heard from others.'
'To put it kindly Inspector I gained the impression that Mr Burgess was inclined, on occasions, to let his mouth rule his brain.'
'In what way sir?'
'To give you an example he told a mutual acquaintance that as I am unmarried and employed a male housekeeper, I must be homosexual. What he might have said if I employed a young woman to fill the same duties I think is best not thought about.'
'One more question sir. Can you tell me if you saw or heard anything unusual between six and seven thirty last evening?
'I am sorry Inspector but that answer to that question has to be no. I expect that you will also wish to know what I was doing at that time ?
'Please sir.'
'I am afraid that I am not going to be able to be of much help. I had my tea at about five forty-five. As I had had a busy day attending the death bed of a parishioner and going into Chichester to deal with certain formalities as she had no living relatives there was quite a lot of correspondence and other parish matters that I need to deal with. Then I said Compline by which time it must have been past seven o'clock. After that I settled down to an evening of reading and listening to a concert on BBC3. Apart from when Harold brought me in a cup of coffee at about nine, I saw nor heard from anyone.'
'So, it would have been possible for you to leave and return to the house unnoticed.'
'Many things are possible in the imagination Inspector. All I can say is that I did not go out.'

'You realise sir this means you have no alibi.'
'I don't suppose I am the only person in that position am I.' he said with a smile. 'Sorry that I can't be of more help.'
He rang a bell on the table and the door opened.
'The inspector is leaving, Harold.'
'I should like a few words with this gentleman if I may', said Love.
'Of course, Harold will show you out. Pleased to have met you Inspector.'
'You know why I am here?' asked Love when the door closed behind the curate.
'The death of Mr Burgess I presume sir.'
'Did you know him?'
'Only by sight sir '
'Did you see or hear anything unusual between six and seven thirty last night ?
'Not that I am able to recall sir.'
'Can you tell me where you were between those hours?'
'His lordship had his tea at five forty-five. When I had cleared up after that meal I sat in my room and read for a short while and then I took a stroll into the village. His lordship had told me he would not require anything until his late evening coffee so I had a couple of hours free. I called in at the Six Bells for a glass of port and returned to the house in time to get his lordship' s coffee at nine.'
'What time did you get to the Six Bells ?'
'Approximately seven thirty and I stayed for about forty-five minutes. When I returned to the house, I had enough time to lock up before getting his lordship his coffee.'
'Why do you refer to your employer as 'his lordship ' ?
'Because, Inspector, he is a peer of the realm and therefore entitled to be addressed as such.'
'Why didn't he tell me that?'
'His lordship does not use his title in connection with parish affairs as it is his right to do.'

Hearing the front door close Donald Craigton came out into the hallway.
'What do you make of Inspector Love, Harold ?'
'He reminds me somewhat of Chief Inspector Wantage my lord' replied Harold with a straight face.
'Now that is an unpleasant thought, 'laughed his employer.

'Any progress Sparrow?' Love asked when he returned to the house.
'We have a couple of people who recall seeing Miss Oakes car passing through the village just after seven thirty.'
'Did any of them recognise the driver?'
'Not enough to say definitely sir. They just assumed it was the lady.'

'What about the knife?'
'No trace of that anywhere sir inside or out. The killer must have taken it with him. How did you get on sir?'
'The only thing I learned, apart from the fact that none of them has an alibi worth noting, is that Burgess seemed to have annoyed or insulted everyone.'
'Enough for one of them to kill him?'
'If you classify trying to get out of paying a bill or calling the local curate gay or falling foul of the Rector's wife who seems to be the queen bee in the place an adequate motive then the answer is no.'
'Sergeant Barnett has started work on the financial side. He is basing himself at the estate agents in Chichester and will report daily.'
'That brings us back to the girl friend. She is the only one with a realistic motive. I want you to find out all you can about her and her business as well as checking out her alibi. For example could she have parked nearby, walked to the house, killed Burgess, got back into her car and drove home to say she discovered him dead? Could she have had an accomplice who either drove the car or did the killing. Concentrate on that line of enquiry.'
'Yes sir '
'Incidentally did the search of the house produce a Will,'
'No sir. I gather that Mr Legge, a solicitor who lives in the village, was his lawyer.'
'I may well call on that gentleman before long. Oh, and Sparrow, have you heard the tale that the curate is a peer?'
'Yes sir, it seems he is Lord Acaster but does not use his title for his church work.'
'Another Tony Benn eh!'
'It seems that everyone in the village is quite happy to go along with his wishes. He is a popular man and well liked.'
'That's as may be but the whole set up seems odd to me. I want you to do some checking Sparrow to see if this story is correct. It wouldn't be the first or the last time someone has assumed a title to which they are not entitled.'
'Very good sir.'
'And Sparrow make some enquiries about the fellow who is the housekeeper for Craigton. He behaves more like a man servant out of a thirties novel than someone living in the eighties.'
'From what I can gather sir he is a bit like a Jeeves or Bunter.'
'And while you are at it check up on the histories of the garden man and those two sisters. Are the stories they are telling true or not? There is something odd about this place and I want it cleared up so that we can concentrate on breaking that alibi.'
'Yes sir.'

'Another thing, Sparrow, get the local man to keep his ear to the ground and report anything useful that is going the rounds. There is nowhere like a small village for gossip.'

Sergeant Alan Barnett had been born the younger son of a father who was the manager of a building company in Norfolk. His mother had been a primary school teacher and was keen to see that her children had a good education. Alan was a hard-working pupil with a great interest in books from an early age. His brother, Adrian, was a more practical child who busied himself with making models. In due course both went on to university, Alan to study economics and Adrian to study engineering. After leaving with a good degree Alan qualified as an accountant and joined one of the big London firms. After a couple of years he began to find the work less and less interesting largely due to the fact that he was always following an audit programme which set out, in considerable detail, what was to be done and how it was to be done and left very little, if any, scope for independent thought. It was this that persuaded Alan to leave accountancy and apply to join the police. He hoped that, in due time, he would be able to join in the investigation of financial crime. His education and accountancy experience ensured his place on a rapid promotion scheme. He had to spend time as a uniformed constable and familiarise himself with the basics of police work. Before log he was promoted to sergeant, the exams posing no great problem for him, and so it was that he found himself posted to the Sussex Police in Chichester to learn how to become a police detective. Out of working hours he was a keen tennis player and also had run a couple of half marathons. Tall, with brown hair and eyes and broad shoulders he was of amiable disposition and generally fitted in well with his colleagues. It was Sergeant Sparrow who told him that he was to undertake an investigation into the financial affairs of Nigel Burgess.

'What we need from you,' said Sparrow 'is information about the finances and the running of Burgess Homes and also information about any other business interests that Burgess had. In essence are the businesses being run properly and what sort of financial picture do they paint. You have been an accountant and should know the sort of thing we are looking for. You are to submit daily reports to the Inspector detailing what you have discovered. Do you think you can manage that and do you need any assistance in doing so? '

'What you are wanting is a form of due diligence report on the businesses this man Burgess was involved in. That should be quite straight forward. I will draw up a programme and see what my enquiries produce.'

'Right. I will contact the new Chief Executive of Burgess Homes and tell him to expect you.'

When Barnett arrived at the head office building for Burgess Homes which was located in an office block on the edge of the city, he was welcomed by Owen Kindle who was the chief accountant of the firm. He was provided with a small office and a chart showing the business structure. Copies of the latest accounts were made available to him as were their accompanying auditors reports. As well as the principal company that ran the estate agency business there were separate companies that dealt with property letting and property management. Owen Kindle also provided Barnett with a copy of the Business operational manuals so that he could see how it was not only structured but also how it was controlled. It was clear that Kindle was running an efficient organisation and was in control of its financial affairs and was able to produce monthly financial reports and annual budgets. With this information Barnett was able to start his own programme. It was quickly clear that the business was not only profitable but had in place an effective management structure. In conversation with Kindle he learned that Burgess also controlled a number of other companies which were his personal investment organisations. Kindle had no direct control over these and they had a small staff of their own and were audited by a local accountancy practice.

In a few days Barnett had gathered sufficient information to allow him to advise his superiors that there appeared to be nothing out of place with the main companies and their allied subsidiaries. When he turned to the private companies, he set about preparing a schedule of the properties that they owned. The list of addresses meant nothing to him but it would be a good idea to make sure that none of them were known to the police for any reason. Having prepared a schedule, he sent it off to County Headquarters with a request for any information they had about the properties. Next, he set out to discover more about these companies and how they operated. He started with their Articles of Association and checked what information had been reported to Companies House about each of them. He noted that, in every case, Nigel Burgess was the managing director and sole shareholder apart from a Walter Legge who was a lawyer and company secretary. Each of the companies appeared to comply with company law and he read the brief entries in their Minutes Books which told him very little apart from what properties were being bought and sold. He studied their accounts and their auditors' reports. Somehow everything seemed too perfect and he found himself becoming suspicious. So, he moved on to the legal documentation reflecting the business of each of the companies. He read the leases for properties that had been bought and then let and it was here that he noticed the first thing that seemed out of place. Looking at one particular lease he sensed that something was different from other leases. A closer examination showed that one of the usual covenants by the tenant was lacking. He made a note of this and found there were others that lacked the same covenant. He made a note of these properties with a view to trying to find out why this was done. Another factor he noted was that in each of these cases the rent to be received was substantially higher than for other and, on the face of it, similar, properties. This raised another interesting question. It became clear from his discussions with the people who worked on these companies that they were really no more than clerks and that all management decisions were taken by Nigel Burgess personally. There was also no common approach in these companies regarding the distribution of profits. Some did pay regular dividends but others seemed to retain all their profits for future investment.

He had found his work both interesting and worthwhile. When he had finished the day's work, he would make his way to his flat in the city, change into casual clothes and go to the tennis club for a couple of sets.

It was at this stage that he received instruction to attend a meeting at the Police Station in Chichester.

CHAPTER 5

By half past eleven in the morning on day after Inspector Love's visit the Private bar at The Six Bells was quite full. All the regulars were there sipping their drinks and sharing notes of the recent events in the village.

 The way that police inspector was going on ' said Olga Sanderson dressed like her sister in a red shirt and white trousers and sipping her gin and tonic ' I can imagine half the village are about to be arrested for lack of a water tight alibi'
'Oh I don't think they arrest people for not having an alibi' replied Trevor Nightingale.
'If they did' added Olivia ' the jails would be full to the brim. Did you have an alibi Trevor?'
'Apparently not one that was good enough for the Inspector. How did you get on Donald?
The curate was in civilian dress as it was his day off and was wearing a plaid shirt and green sweater with cord trousers.
'I gathered I failed the test as well. Mind you I would imagine that ninety per cent of the village would be in the same position. Lack of an alibi does not, as I understand it, equate with being a suspect. At least not in every case.'
'Yes, but who did do it?' cried Olga. 'Someone must have killed the man.'
'I shouldn't think he was short of enemies if his behaviour in general was anything like it was in the village 'replied Trevor.
'The police will want to find out why before they can decide on who' added Olivia.
'You sound like a TV pundit on crime and criminals darling' laughed her sister.
'I repeat what I said before he died 'said Trevor, 'From what I have heard he has not been above using doubtful means for obtaining the authorisations that some of his deals needed.'
'Do you mean bribing people ?' asked Donald.
'How he has done it I don't know. What I do know is that some of his schemes were odds on against until he came on to the scene. If the police want to find out who killed him, I think they should concentrate on his business affairs rather than his personal relationships with people in this village.'
'I imagine they will look at both 'said Donald.
'If it was connected to his business affairs 'Trevor went on 'It means that someone must have come into the village, killed him and got away again. We don't get many strangers here so they should be more noticeable.'
'The police are doing that ' said Olga
'How do you know ? her sister asked.
'When I went into the shop this morning I heard that the police had been making door to door calls to ask that very question.'

'Of course', said Donald 'its possible that whoever it was came over the Downs and not through the village.'
'That's right' agreed Trevor. 'The Burgess palace is at the very end of the village. Someone could approach the house from outside and the odds are they wouldn't be seen.'
'On the other hand' said Olivia ' I suppose it could have been some deranged person who didn't even know Burgess.'
'The passing lunatic is not a very likely option I should have thought' pointed out Donald.
'If it was someone connected to his business activities then the field is going to be much wider.' Said Trevor
'Could it be a contract killing?' asked Olivia.
'That sort of thing only happens on TV not in Upper Burford' laughed Trevor.' Let's hope the police soon make some progress.'
'And leave us in peace 'said Olga.
'I agree entirely darling 'added her sister

At this point the door opened and Megan Legg entered with her dog Rufus.

'Megan 'cried Olga 'we don't often see you here. Have you come to confess?'
'Confess 'Megan almost shrieked 'confess to what?'
'Take no notice of her darling 'said Olivia. 'We were just talking about the death of the Burgess man.'
'It's not really a joke 'said Megan.'
'No its not 'said Trevor 'let me get you a drink. What will it be?'
'A dry sherry please Trevor.'
'It may be funny to you Olga but I think that policeman thinks I did it.'
'Why on earth should he do that?' asked Donald.
'Because he told me that I had no alibi. And because I had taken Rufus for a walk and had just started up the lane when he thought he saw a rabbit and disappeared into the undergrowth. It took me nearly a quarter of an hour to get him back on his lead and, as a result, I was late getting to the Historical Society lecture in Chichester.'
'Is that all darling? 'asked Olga. 'Then you are in same position as everyone else here. None of us have an Inspector Love proof alibi.'
'Did Rufus catch his rabbit?' asked Trevor
'Of course not. Any rabbit could outrun him. Its just that I have never been questioned by the police before and it made me nervous.'
'No-one in his right mind is going to suspect you Megan 'said Trevor.
'Of course he isn't ' added Olivia patting her on the arm.
'Did you see anything or hear anything unusual Megan ?' Donald asked.

'The Inspector asked me that but I didn't hear or see anything. Besides I was totally preoccupied with catching Rufus. He's a bad boy 'she said patting the dog who wagged his tail.
'Rabbit Rufus 'Olivia called and the dog got to is feet and started to bark.'
'Behave yourself Rufus, 'said his owner 'and sit down and be quiet.'
'You shouldn't tease him 'chided Olga. 'You know what he is like about rabbits.'
At the sound of the word Rufus started to bark again and everyone dissolved into laughter. Shortly after Megan left scolding her dog for being a bad boy.
'If Love thinks she did it I don't give much for his chances of catching the real killer' said Trevor.
'I know', agreed Olga 'look at her the poor dear. The typical village spinster dressed in best JS fashions. No wonder it took her so long to catch Rufus I shouldn't think she could catch a bus.'
'What are JS fashions? 'asked Donald.
'Jumble Sale 'laughed Olivia. 'The poor darling always looks as if that is where she buys her clothes.

CHAPTER 6

Richard Buxton looked out of the window of his lounge, over the roofs of Kemptown in Brighton and out on to the English Channel. As a man born and brought up in London it was a view of which he never tired. Once again, he thought how much Doreen, his wife who had died of cancer just before his transfer to the Sussex force would have loved living by the seaside. With a sigh he went to the kitchen and prepared his breakfast. At eight fifteen he extracted his car from the underground parking of the apartment block and drove into Hove to the county police headquarters in a new glass and concrete building. Once at his desk he read through the reports that had come in over night updating him on the various cases the serious crime squad were investigating. He was particularly interested in that from Inspector Love in Chichester who was leading the Burgess investigation. Buxton found Love's reports full of facts and short of ideas. It was clear the man was a plodder who followed well defined avenues of investigation. So far, they were still at the information gathering stage. Love's latest report did not show any clear light on who might have killed the businessman although it was plain, he fancied the ex girl friend as the most likely candidate. At this point his telephone rang.

'Chief Superintendent the AC asks if you could spare him a few minutes, 'a female voice enquired.
'I will be with him asap 'Buxton replied.

Assistant Chief Constable Jonathon Cantrill was on the phone but pointed to a chair inviting Buxton to take a seat.
'Good morning Richard'
'Good morning sir.'
' How is the Burgess case getting on? Any sign of an arrest yet?'
'Not yet sir. We are still digging into the deceased's life and business activities. Things may be clearer when we have done that.'
'Keep me posted.'
'Yes sir.'
'The Chief has asked me to hand this on to you' the AC passed a letter over the desk. Attached to it was note in the Chief's hand which said "Keep this woman out of my hair"
Buxton looked at the letter which was written in green ink and seemed to be complaining about the actions of the police in Upper Burford.
' The Chief was on the same working party as this woman and had his fill of her on that occasion. You had better deal with it and see if you can quieten her down. It seems she is the daughter of a bishop and has inflated ideas as to her own importance. Having read the epistle all I can add is – good luck.'

Back at his desk Buxton read the letter which was written in green ink. The writer, using her association with the Chief Constable, wanted to lodge a complaint about Inspector Love who it seemed in questioning various leading citizens in the village had virtually accused them of being involved with the death of Nigel Burgess on the grounds that they did not have a provable alibi. Indeed, he had gone so far as to suggest this very fact to the writer herself who, as the Chief Constable knew, was the daughter of a bishop. Buxton put the letter aside and buzzed for his administrative assistant to come in.
'Read that Toby' he said and added 'I have never understood why the clergy and their spouses always write letters of complaint in green ink.'
'It seems Love is lacking in diplomatic skills' Toby laughed.'
'What do we know about him?' Buxton asked.' I have not come across one his cases before.'
'Love? He's an efficient officer with quite a good record. Not the brightest star in the sky. Works very much according to the book. Seems to lack much in the way of imagination '
'It looks as if I am going to have to pay a visit to Inspector Love and then go and try and pour oil on the water at Burford Rectory. Is there anything you want me for?'
'This came in this morning. Its an enquiry from Love's team asking if we know anything about various properties in companies controlled by the deceased. It come from a Sergeant Barnett who is on secondment to Chichester as part of the rapid training programme. Before joining the force, he was an accountant with JCDR in London. It seems Love has put him on to the case. '
'Right, I will take this down to Vice and Drug to see if they have any information. I want a word with Bill Underhill anyway.'

Chief Inspector Bill Underhill was a short thick man with grizzled grey hair. He was known as being a dedicated fighter against the drug trade due in part, it was said, because his own daughter had died of an overdose foisted on her at a party.
'Good morning Bill 'Buxton greeted him.
'Morning sir. Can I help or is this a courtesy call?'
'I am not sure if you know anything about the Burgess case Bill.'
'The estate agent who was knifed to death?'
'That's the one. I have received a request from the officer looking into his finances asking if we know anything about the properties listed here. It seems they are assets of companies controlled by Burgess.'
Underhill took the list and cast his eye down it.
'Nothing jumps off the page' he said 'but I will get someone to go through the list just to make sure.'
'While they are doing that perhaps we could have a word about the Gorleston case.'

'The two men spent some time discussing the case of a drug ring that the police were trying to bust. A uniformed constable brought in a computer print out and handed it to Underhill.'

'That list of properties you were asking about sir ' he said and withdrew.

Underhill looked at the printout and raised an eyebrow.

'Interesting 'he said and passed the printout across the desk.

Against each of the addresses there was a code number.

'What does this mean Bill?'

'Those marked with a zero means we have no information about them. Those marked with a 5 indicate that the property is known to us. The number five means it is a property believed to be used in the sex trade,'

'A brothel, do you mean?'

'Not necessarily a brothel more likely a massage parlour. We may know about the property and its usage but, to be honest, we don't have the resources to close them down or to make charges against those running them. Every now and then we raid one or two just to see if the girls working there are not illegal immigrants. If they are, we seek to deport them and to charge whoever is in charge with running a disorderly house. Mind you, we have hardly closed one when another will open.'

'So it appears that the late Mr Burgess was involved in the sex trade.'

'I doubt if he was directly involved sir. The usual approach is that the owner of the property leases it to some other person and they are the one who runs the massage parlour. There is nothing to suggest the owner knew what was going on. However, that does not mean that he does not do very nicely thank you from the sky-high rent charged for the property.'

'How to get rich without getting your hands dirty.'

'You could say that.'

'Well, thanks for this info Bill. If you pick up anything interesting about any of these places perhaps you will let me know.'

Buxton drove over to Chichester and had lunch at the restaurant in the cathedral cloisters before making his way to the police headquarters where he asked for Inspector Love. The Inspector was busy on some of his routine work when the door opened and Sergeant Sparrow entered.

'What is it Sparrow? Can't you see I am busy? Have you made any progress on that alibi yet?'

'Not yet sir. It's just that Chief Superintendent Buxton is asking to speak with you.'

'Well put him through man.'

'He's not on the phone sir he's here talking to the Super.'

'What's he doing here, all my reports have gone to HQ haven't they?'

'Yes sir. Shall I show him in?'

'Very well and you had better arrange some tea and biscuits.'
'Very good sir.'
A minute later the door opened again and Sparrow' voice announced,
'Chief Superintendent Buxton sir.'

Love got to his feet and greeted his superior officer with guarded politeness.'
'Any special reason for this visit sir?' he asked when the formalities were
completed.
'You won't be surprised to hear it is about the Burgess case.'
'The investigation is proceeding satisfactorily sir as I think you will have seen
from my reports.'
'There are a couple of things I can add to those reports Inspector. First, you
might read this.'
He handed over the letter from Mrs Trumper minus the note from the Chief
Constable.'
'What's your comment on that? 'he asked.'
'I completely reject the assertions she is making sir. I did question a number of
people in the village with a view of trying to find out more about the deceased
and his relationship with the local inhabitants. All of them seemed to have
crossed swords with Burgess at one time or another and had a possible motive.
Naturally I asked each of them where they had been at the relevant time. The
thing was that none of them had an alibi that was worth a cup of cold tea. If I
remarked on that it was not to suggest that they were a suspect but to draw their
attention to their position.'
'I see. Well the Chief has asked me to deal with the letter and I wanted to get
your reaction to it before I did so.'
'That Mrs Trumper seems to be the queen bee in the village sir and, frankly, has
an inflated idea of her importance.'
'Well you certainly appear to have disturbed the hive, Inspector. Tell me, how
many murders have you investigated?'
'This is the third sir. The other two were successfully solved.'
'Well done. I think you had better leave any future contacts with these people
to me. Now for something that you will not know. Your Sergeant Barnett asked
HQ if we had any information about a number of properties held in companies
controlled by Burgess. This is the list and you will see that some of them have a
number five by the address. That means the property has been identified as
being used in the sex trade, as massage parlours rather than brothels. There are
three in Brighton and Hove, two in Crawley and one each in Worthing,
Horsham and St Leonards. '
'So Burgess was running these places was he?'
'I doubt it. His company or companies own the property which is most likely
leased out at a very high rent to the people who actually run the business. A nice
earner and he can always deny he knew to what use the property is being used.

This means we are going to have to widen our enquiries beyond Upper Burford.'
'We are already doing that sir. I have set in motion an investigation into Burgess' business affairs.' Love almost smirked with self righteousness. 'However, to my mind we are most likely to find the party we want is the ex girl friend. A woman scorned may be somewhat of an obvious answer but its often the right one.'
'I thought she had an alibi ?'
'We are putting that through the mill sir. If we can break it, I think we will have our perpetrator.'
'Very well, Inspector, keep me posted with daily reports please. I shall be particularly interested in any further reports from Sergeant Barnett. He seems like a bright young man.'
This last remark clearly did not appeal to Inspector Love.
'Oh, by the way,' added Buxton 'do you know a Walter Legg a local solicitor?'
'Yes sir he is a very well know man in the city.'
'I gather he was Burgess' lawyer. I think I will go and have a word with him while I am here. I will let you know what he has to say.'

The offices of Legg, Davies and Legg were in a Georgian property almost opposite the cathedral. Buxton was only kept waiting about five minutes in a comfortably furnished waiting room before being shown into a large room with an enormous window that overlooked a courtyard garden in the centre of which was a walnut tree. In front of the window stood a very large desk behind which was seated a man in his early sixties. He was just over medium height had a round face with brown eyes and his hair, which was cut very short sought to reduce the effect of his hair loss. He wore a charcoal grey double breasted suit, a pale blue shirt and a college tie. He stretched out a well manicured hand.

'Chief Superintendent I am delighted to meet you' the voice was as smooth as silk. 'Please make yourself comfortable and tell me how I can be of assistance.'
'I understand sir that your firm represented the late Mr Nigel Burgess both in a business and in a personal capacity.'
'That is indeed the case. His untimely death in that fashion is nothing less than a tragedy.'
'As I am sure you appreciate Mr Legg when it is necessary to investigate a death of this nature it is very important to learn as much as possible as quickly as possible about the deceased. Without prejudicing your professional codes, I am hoping you may be able to help in this enquiry. '
'I shall be happy to do what I can Chief Superintendent.'
'To date we have been unable to trace whether he had any relatives living.'

'I can easily answer that question. He had no next of kin of any degree. He was the only child of parents who were themselves only children. As far as I am aware there were no second or even third cousins.'

'I understand. Tell me, had you known Mr Burgess for a long time?'

'I first met him when he opened his original agency in the city and he approached me to act for him in matters relating to the lease. '

'Do you happen to know anything about his life before that point?'

'Over the years and through many meetings, lunches and dinners with him I learned he had been born and brought up in south London. His first job was as a sales representative for firm of estate agents in Croydon. That was when he studied to be a chartered surveyor. It was when he left that firm and then set up on his own that he came to this city. From that modest beginning he was successful in building a group of estate agencies and property companies of one type or another until he became both successful and wealthy.'

'Can you think of anyone, sir, who might wish him harm ?'

'A man like Nigel Burgess who has built a business empire from scratch does not do so, Chief Superintendent, without incurring the disappointment and even the displeasure of some of his rivals in business. Having said that I find it hard to believe that anyone would be constrained to make a physical attack on him.'

'I believe that you live in the same village as Mr Burgess?'

'Yes, I was born in the house I still occupy with my unmarried sister. I was the person who identified the building opportunity afforded by an old barn on the edge of the village and mentioned it to Nigel. I don't know if you have seen the property now, Chief Superintendent, but if you have you will appreciate what a wonderful conversion has been achieved to create what is, without a doubt, the finest house in the village.

'How did Mr Burgess settle into life in the village, sir ?'

'I would be less than honest if I said everything went smoothly from day one. Nigel Burgess had never lived in a small community before especially one with such a long and generally unchanging history as Upper Burford. He was, by nature, a man who was always looking forward and seeing fresh opportunities. A self-made man he had little sympathy with some of more traditional ways you still find in village life. But he was settling down and would soon have settled comfortably into local society.'

'A final question if I may Mr Legg. Are you able to give me any information as to who will benefit materially from his death?'

'Ah yes, the Will, 'Walter Legg rubbed his hands together. 'The full details will I think have to wait until after the funeral. However, I think I can say that his Will leaves a number of pecuniary legacies but the principal beneficiaries are charities. I think you will agree, from that brief comment, that it is unlikely that anyone killed him for what they might gain from his death.'

'The estate is substantial?'

'I expect it to be several hundreds of thousands.'

CHAPTER 7

Before returning to Brighton Buxton decided to go at look at the scene of the crime.   The Big Barn was indeed a luxurious house with expensive and tasteful furnishings. He was shown around by the sergeant who was protecting the property from unwanted visitors. There was little to be seen as far as the scene of the crime was concerned. The garden chair was still in its place even though it was covered by a plastic sheet which was taped in place. He looked at the two exits and went a short way into the copse and down the path to the road. The detailed search had been concluded and nothing of interest had been found. However, it allowed Buxton to get the location fixed in his mind. Leaving the house, he decided to have a stroll around the village to get a feel of the place. As he was passing the church, he noticed that the door opened and a man came out of the building. He was tall and slender and had grey hair. It was only when he turned to walk down the path towards the street that Buxton realised that it was someone, he thought he knew.
'Father?' he called out.'
The man stopped and looked hard at him and then broke into a smile and hurried to the lychgate.
'Richard Buxton he extended a hand and shook the other's warmly. 'It's a long time since I saw you. How are you and what are you doing in rural Sussex ?'
'I am fine thank-you Father. As a matter of fact, I am here on business.'
'They've not called in the Yard on this Burgess affair, have they? Otherwise what brings a DI from the Met here on business?'
'I am not with the Met nowadays. Here you had better see my ID.'
'Chief Superintendent no less and Head of the Serious Crime Unit. A well deserved promotion. '
'More to point what are you doing here Father? All we ever knew was that you had taken early retirement'
'Sorry Richard but I wonder if you would mind not calling me Father which was after all just a nickname at the Yard. Please call me Donald'
'Apologies, force of habit I suppose. What's the matter with it anyway? Will people think you are my dad? '
'I hope I don't look that old' the other laughed. 'No its because of this.'

He pulled back the scarf he was wearing to reveal a clerical collar.
'If people hear you calling me Father, they will think I have gone over to Rome
'he grinned.
'Are you saying you are a vicar?' Buxton gasped.
'Not at all. I am merely a curate.'
'I would never have thought it' Buxton shook his head. 'I never saw you as
clergy material.'
'Just shows how wrong you can be. Look, I live nearby, come and have a cup
of tea and a chat.'
He led the way a short distance and through an impressive gateway and up a
path to a large red brick and timber house. Just as he was getting out a key to
open the door was opened by very neatly dressed man in a blue suit and a white
shirt and quiet tie.
'By all that's wonderful 'Buxton cried ' its Holy Harry.'
'Not any more Richard.' admonished Donald,' Nowadays its Harold
Whitehouse. 'Here's an old friend Harold.'
'Chief Inspector Buxton! Delighted to see you again sir.'
'Not just Chief Inspector Harold it's now Chief Superintendent of the Sussex
Police.'
'A well merited promotion I am sure sir.'
Buxton followed his host into the house and the door was closed behind him by
Harold Whitehouse.
'I think tea and some of your fruit cake is called for Harold.'
'Very good my lord. Will you take it in the lounge?'
'No I don't think so let's go into the study.'
The study had book lined walls, a window on to the garden and a large desk
covered in papers. There was also two leather armchairs and a coffee table.
'Make yourself at home Richard' said his friend and pointed to one of the chairs
and then sat himself in the other.
'What is going on here Donald? I come to a small village and find a former CDI
from the Yard in clerical garb. He brings me to what he says is his house, a
property worth far more than any copper could afford and what do I find. The
door is opened by a man with a record as long as my arm. A record of
confidence tricks where he pretended to be a senior church official.'
'You are a classic copper Richard ' Donald laughed ' always assume a man is
guilty until he can prove he had nothing to do with the crime.'
At this point the door opened and Harold Whitehouse entered carrying a tray
containing tea things and a slices of fruit cake.'
'We will look after ourselves Harold thank you'
'Very good my lord'.
"And that's another thing' said Buxton 'why does he call you my lord? I repeat.
What is going on here?'
'Alright Richard don't get over excited 'Donald said passing him a cup of tea

' and have a slice of cake. I think you will find its pretty good. The answer to
your question starts with the man in the picture.'
Richard followed his pointing finger and looked at the portrait over the fireplace
which was of a man dressed in a black coat and waistcoat, a white shirt with a
butterfly collar, a grey tied and striped trousers. On his feet were black shoes
and spats. He appeared to be about sixty years of age.
'That is my great uncle Ernest Harold Akehurst, the only surviving child of the
owner of a small shop in a village outside Leeds. He was always a bright lad
and won scholarships to Leeds County Grammar School and then to St Johns
College, Cambridge where he got a double first in law and economics. He
qualified as a solicitor, joined the biggest firm in Leeds and became in time not
just a partner but the senior partner. Among his clients were some of the biggest
trade unions in the area. In due course he stood for the city council, was elected
and later was made an alderman, then served his year as Lord Mayor. In 1924
he entered parliament as a labour member for a Leeds constituency. Ramsay
Macdonald led a short-lived labour government and then the party went into
opposition. Great uncle became a shadow spokesman on Home Office affairs.
In 1929 when Macdonald won a second term, he joined the government as a
home office minister. When the crash came in 1931, he stayed loyal to
Macdonald and was rewarded by being made a peer and a government
spokesman on Home Office business in the upper chamber. He was now the
first Baron Acaster in County of Yorkshire. When Macdonald retired and was
succeeded by Baldwin great uncle lost his position and ceased to play an active
part in politics. He held quite a range of company directorships including being
the deputy chairman of a bank. He had bought this house, that had been
designed by Lutyens, when he became a government minister. Ernest had
married a Yorkshire girl and they had two children, my uncle Basil and my
mother Grace. Basil was a chip off the old block and had a considerable
intellect. He took a double first in Oxford, this time it was Biology and Botany,
became a lecturer, then a professor of Research Botany and stayed in Oxford for
the rest of his life. He was a charming man but an archetypal scholar. He never
married. My mother did marry and had three children. My elder brother Simon
became a chartered accountant with one of the big London firms. He married
and had three daughters. I was the second born and to some degree followed my
great uncle into law except that I joined the Metropolitan Police. My sister,
Rosemary, became an Anglican nun and has been working in India for a good
many years. As you know I never married. If things had gone according to plan
Simon would inherit the title when Uncle Basil died, but sadly he dropped dead
on the golf course before any of his daughters could marry and produce a son.
This meant that for a while at least I became the heir to the title. Fate played its
last trick by allowing Uncle Basil to catch a chill while on a field trip in Norway
which turned into pneumonia and that carried off the old boy. Suddenly I found
myself the third baron. To be frank I did not welcome being a titled detective

and the butt of Met humour nor did I fancy being cross examined by some smart
barrister as Lord Acaster. '
'Couldn't you have resigned the peerage à la Tony Benn? 'asked Buxton
'I could possibly have done that but I didn't out of respect for my great uncle.
Then I found that as well as the title I inherited this place for life and the income
from a not inconsiderable trust fund. This meant that, if I took early retirement,
together with my Met pension I would have no financial worries. It also, and
more importantly, meant that I could bring forward my retirement plan. For
years I had planned to enter the church when I retired. I had been a licensed
Reader for some twenty years.'
'I never knew that.'
'There was no reason why you should. So, I took early retirement and applied
for ordination. After that I expected to become an NSM.'
'What is an NSM ,'
'A Non-Stipendiary Minister or, in other words an amateur priest. One who is
not paid a stipend. They usually deputise for priests who are ill, or during an
interregnum or on a sabbatical. However, just before my ordination the bishop
told me he wanted me to become the curate in this parish. Normally it would not
warrant a curate but it so happens that our Rector is a world expert on ancient
Greek drama and is much in demand at conferences and seminars which leaves
him insufficient time to do all that is need to run a parish. An NSM curate
would be the ideal solution. So, there you are, young Richard, that is how I
came to be the curate here and am wearing a clerical collar. It is also why I am
called my lord by Harold although I do not use the title in my church role,
preferring to be known simply as the Reverend Donald Craigton. And by the
way, 'he added with a smile, 'you will find all that is confirmed when you have
a check up made on what I have told you.'
'But what about Holy Harry? How does he fit in?'
'When I was in training, I did some prison visiting. One day I was asked to see
a prisoner who was seeking help. It was Harold Whitehouse. When we got over
our mutual surprise, he told me he had decided he had spent too long as guest of
Her Majesty and that the time had come to go straight. He wanted help to find a
home and a job. When we talked about his life I discovered he had spent some
years in the RAF as a young man and had been employed in the officers mess
which gave him a variety of experience from silver service waiting to acting as
a sort of batman and even to being a more than average cook. When I was
trying to work out how best to help him it occurred to me that, as a full-time
curate, I was going to need help to run this house. I offered Harold a six-month
trial. He accepted and its proved to be a considerable success for both of us. I
have the help I need and he has a home and a job. He has settled in very well to
village life. He sings in the church choir on Sunday and is popular in the bar of
the Six Bells. You know, Richard, he is just like an actor he needs to hide
behind the part he is playing. That is why he was so good as a con man and its

why he is now playing a Jeeves cum Bunter part. And there you have the complete story apart from the fact that, as far as the village is concerned, I worked for the Home Office before entering the church. I do not mention in what capacity.'

'It's going to be a great help having an ex Yard man in the village ' Buxton said.'

'Now, just a minute Richard, 'Donald said in a stern voice. 'My duty here is the care of the souls of the parishioners. I will not become a copper's nark. So, if you were thinking you had a spy in the village you can think again. I will do my duty as any citizen should but I will not break what is called the secrecy of the confession. Understood?'

'Understood. But that does not prevent you telling me what you made of Nigel Burgess.'

'You will have seen what Inspector Love noted from our interview.'

'I have read his report but …'

'You were not impressed? 'Donald asked with a grin.'

'Not particularly.'

'Harold said he reminded him of Inspector Wantage.'

'That's certainly a name from the past that I prefer to forget. But, seriously, what did you make of Burgess?'

'I did not have a lot to do with him. When I called, he showed me the door in pretty quick time. He was, I believe, a fairly typical self-made businessman who thought that money provided him with power. He had no idea about how life in a small village panned out and he didn't take the time to play himself into Upper Burford. The result was he managed to upset pretty well everyone.'

'Seriously enough for one of them to want to top him ?'

'I shouldn't have thought so. However, as you well know, no-one can ever say with complete certainty what may cause someone to act for a reason that would seem totally out of proportion.'

'You think that might be true in this case ?'

'I have no idea. It was just a thought. Successful men like Burgess are not usually short of people whom they have outwitted or has done the dirty on. You will probably have quite a wide field.'

'Inspector Love seems to favour the girl friend who was just about to leave the house.'

'That would be about par for the course with a man like Love.'

'It's been a pleasure to meet up with you again Donald.' Buxton got to his feet

'Yes, we must keep in touch in a nonprofessional way.'

'Now I must go and see your rector's wife. It seems that Love managed to upset her enough for her to write to the Chief.'

'That doesn't surprise me. Verity sees herself as the leader of social life in the village now there is no squire. She means well, its just that sometimes she can come the lady bountiful it bit too much. I wouldn't mind being a fly on the wall at your meeting.'

Buxton was shown into the lounge at The Rectory where Mrs Trumper was seated in an armchair. She did not rise to greet him nor did she invite him to sit down. He had feeling that she thought he should have called at the back door like any tradesman. When he had introduced himself and the reason for his call she said in an icy tone;
'I should have hoped that the Chief Constable would have replied personally to my letter particularly as we have served on an important committee together.'
'He regrets that he is unable to do that madam, due to pressure of work. That is why he asked me, as the senior officer in this matter, to call and to give you his reply in person.'
'I trust that means that Inspector Love has been reprimanded as to his behaviour.'
Buxton chose to ignore that remark.
'It is most unfortunate that Inspector Love, who is an experienced officer, should have inadvertently given the impression that the absence of an independently supported alibi meant that anyone was suspected of being involved in the case. In matters of this nature it is both important and useful to the police to ask those known to the deceased what their movements were for the time in question. The reason why this is done is to help us complete what may be described as a jigsaw puzzle that gives a picture of the locality of the investigation. Let me put it this way. If the police ask, let us say, ten people where they were and what they were doing then that information could possibly help them in interpreting details that they have gained from other sources. For example it can make it clear that all of those people were in no way near the scene of the crime and could not have seen or heard anything germane to the enquiry. The fact that any of them did not have what may be described as a checkable alibi is not in itself an indication that they are considered as other than someone who knew the deceased. In fact, I should expect to find that the majority of us would find it hard if not impossible to provide a checkable alibi for every moment of our lives. The fact is, Mrs Trumper, that sometimes the answers to those standard questions lead to something that can be of real assistance to the investigators. That is why they have to be asked. Whilst Inspector Love was correct to point out to an interviewee that they did not have a checkable alibi, it is unfortunate that he does not seem to have clarified the fact that those circumstances did not mean that the person is to be viewed with suspicion. To that end I would ask you to accept the apologies of the Force and to assure you that Inspector Love asks that this oversight be corrected.'
'Well of course I accept the apology the Chief Constable has required you to make on his behalf. I just hope that Inspector Love will choose his words with greater care in future. This village has never been the scene of a murder, as I

know to my certain knowledge. The man Burgess was a quite deplorable
person. Indeed, I have heard suggestions that certain of his transactions whilst
not overtly illegal may well have been morally reprehensible. I should think the
police would better occupy their time looking at his business activities rather
than submitting the law-abiding citizens of this village to inappropriate
examination.'
'Are you able to give me any more information as to the source of those
statements or the nature of the matters to which they refer?'
'Certainly not. That is the job for which the police are paid.'

Buxton could see no reason to continue the discussion and took a polite leave of
a lady who clearly had inflated ideas as to her own importance.

CHAPTER 8

'You will need to turn left in just over a mile sir' said Sergeant David Grant.
'You seem very familiar with this area Sergeant 'replied Inspector Robert Thomasson.
'I have a wife who is a Guider and a daughter who is a Brownie so I am well indoctrinated.'
'Does that mean you know the place we are heading for ?'
'I have been there before sir. It's an official Guide Camp of the Sussex Guide Association. They can camp there or hold Brownie Pack Holidays in a specially adapted building. It covers about four acres I would think a mixture of trees and clearings. There's a lane about a hundred yards on the right and then a gate into the site almost immediately after the turning.'

A uniformed police officer was at the gate and saluted.

'The site office is about forty yards from the car park sir. Sergeant Simpson is there with the lady who says she is the site warden.'
'Thank you, constable. Has the pathologist arrived yet?'
'About five minutes ago sir.'

They parked the car and entered the brick built single story building that bore a sign saying "Camp Bureau". Inside they found the police sergeant and a woman PC together with a middle-aged lady who Thomasson took to be the Warden.

'Where's the doctor?' he asked.
'A constable has taken him to where the body was found sir.'
'Right' he introduced himself to the lady and said he would come and talk with her in a short while. Then, accompanied by Sergeants Grant and Simpson he went along a path and through the trees until they came to a small clearing in which there were a number of rows of benches. At the far end was what was obviously meant to be an altar with a wooden cross standing on it. The police constable and the pathologist were standing and looking at a figure that laid on the ground.

'Morning Inspector 'called Dr Oscar Penrose. 'I thought I would leave touching anything until you arrived.'

Thomasson and Grant moved forward to look down at what had been a woman in her sixties. Her hair, which was all they could see, was steely grey. She was wearing a bottle green sweatshirt and black trousers and hiking boots. At that moment two more police officers arrived.

'Get us some pictures of the body and the surroundings. You made sure she was dead doctor?'
'Yes, but that was confirmed by the local GP who has had to dash to a confinement. 'He gave an estimate of death about ten to twelve hours ago.'
'Do we know who she is Simpson?'
'Not yet sir.'
'Right then it's over to you doctor.'

The doctor spent some minutes examining the body.

'Is it alright to turn her over?'
'I don't see why not.'

Having allowed a few more minutes Thomasson asked
'What can you tell me? '
' Cause of death seems quite simple a knife was driven into her back and straight into the left ventricle. Death would have been instantaneous. I don't suppose she knew anything about it. Whoever did this was either an expert with a knife or just plain lucky. There's not much more I can do here. Get her body over to the mortuary and I will do the post mortem this evening or tomorrow morning. You'll get my report as soon as possible after that.'

The doctor stood up and brushed the knees of his trousers. As he made to leave he turned and spoke to Thomasson.

'Rather a coincidence, but I had another case with similar cause of death recently.' And with a wave of his hand set off through the trees.
'What's that she has round her waist sergeant? 'he asked Grant who knelt down and then said 'it looks like a money belt.'
'Get a picture of it and then take it off so we can see what is inside.'

They opened the purse on the altar. It contained a smaller notecase in which there was some notes and several cards as well as a driving licence. The licence was issued to an Audrey Marie Hope and the photo left little doubt it was the deceased. In one of the pockets was a card giving not only her name but her address and telephone number. More scene of crime officers had arrived and Thomasson, having instructed Sergeant Simpson to arrange for the body to be removed, returned to the building.

'You are? 'he asked the middle-aged lady
'My name is Iris Agar and I am the part time warden at this site. This is a terrible thing to happen in a place like this Inspector.'

'It seems Mrs Agar' Thomasson had noticed the wedding ring 'that the lady was a Audrey Marie Hope. Did you know her?'

'I have never heard of her but that's not unlikely seeing how many people there were her last evening.'

'Why was that madam?'

'It was the annual camp fire and barbecue evening of the county FG2 and there must have been at least eighty people present.'

'Do you have a list of their names?.'

'Certainly not. The event was arranged by the county committee for the FG2. They are the only ones who would have that information.'

'You mention FG2 Mrs Agar. What exactly is that?

' It stands for Former Guides and Former Guiders, two sets of the initials F and G which became FG2.'

'Thank you. Now can you tell me exactly what did happen here last evening?'

'It was an annual event attended by members of FG2 in the county. They come here to have a camp fire singalong and a barbecue. Not that they cook the food themselves. That is done by outside caterers. It started at about seven thirty and ended at about ten. Most of the ladies arrived by car and left the same way.'

'And no-one reported that Audrey Hope was missing?

'No. After they had gone, I shut the main gate and locked it. This morning I did my usual tour of the site just to make certain that everything was in order. It was then I noticed a car still in the car park. I assumed it must have broken down and that the owner would arrange for it to be collected today. It was during my tour that I looked in at the chapel and there she was laying on the floor. I couldn't waken her so I phoned 999. That is all I know Inspector. Now, if you have finished with me I have quite a lot to do. There is brownie pack holiday and three guide patrol camps arriving this afternoon.'

'I am sorry Mrs Agar but that will not be possible.'

'What do you mean its not possible.'

'This is a crime scene. The lady has been stabbed to death. The site is closed to all comers until the police have completed their thorough search of the whole site.'

'That will have to wait until after the weekend.'

'I am sorry but we cannot allow a whole group of people adults and children to have use of the site until we have completed our enquiries.'

'But they will have made all their arrangements, sorted out camping gear, bought food and notified parents. You can't simply turn them away at the gate.'

'I appreciate the problems madam but this site is closed for the time being.'

'This is impossible! I shall report your attitude to the County Commissioner who will not doubt inform the Chief Constable of your arrogant behaviour'

With this she swept into the back room and slammed the door.

'She'll get over it' said Thomasson. 'Now Grant you are the Guiding expert how do we go about finding who organised last night's bean feast?'

'I think I saw a County Handbook on the shelf sir. Yes, here it is. With any luck this should tell us who runs this FG2 and they should be able to tell us who was here last night.'
'Get on to that straight away. I want to know how we are going to get names and addresses. Oh, and who did the catering. I am going to look at the car.'

The car was Ford and was some years old. The keys had been found in the bag round the waist. Thomasson had taken Simpson with him. They opened the driver's door but could not see anything out of the ordinary. It was the same with the passenger door. Being a two-door model, they folded the front seats but found nothing in the back apart from a car rug. When they opened the boot the found a handbag, a pair of shoes and an anorak.

'Let's get some photos of this 'Thomasson said and then bring the bag and anything else you find to the Bureau.
Back at the building he asked Grant how he was progressing.

'It's not going to be easy sir ' he replied ' I have spoken to the County Secretary but she hasn't got a list of attendees. It will be necessary to contact each of the individual group secretaries to obtain the information we want. I have arranged for a local officer to pick up the names and addresses of those local people and we will then have to contact them one by one.'
'Why did you say we wanted this information ?'
'I said there had been a fatality at the site and we needed to know if any of those who attended had not arrived home safely. '
'That should stop too much speculation. I have looked at the car and all I found was a handbag and a pair of shoes plus an anorak. We have got her address so I think the next thing to do is go to the house.'

Audrey Hope had lived in a semi-detached Victorian villa in Emsworth. Before entering the house, Thomasson asked the neighbours either side when they had last seen Miss Hope. He was told that no-one had seen her since the day before. Taking the key Thomasson opened the front door and entered a narrow hallway from which stairs led up to the first floor. There were two doors on the left-hand side and one at the end of the hallway. This led into a kitchen which was neat and tidy. Some washing up was drying on the draining board and a basket of laundry was waiting to be sorted out. The main room on the ground floor was a lounge/dining room. What had originally been two rooms had had the wall knocked down to create a single unit. Apart from the usual furniture there were some bookshelves which appeared to contain a good many books, a television and a music centre with a cupboard filled with records and tapes. There was also a bureau which contained private papers and a small filing cabinet which housed a number of named files one of which was entitled 'Will'. Thomasson opened that and saw that the document was in an envelope bearing the name of a local firm of solicitors. Upstairs were two bedrooms and a bathroom none of which showed any signs of items other than would be expected. On a chest of drawers in the main bedroom there stood a photograph of a woman in Guide Uniform. There was no doubt that it was the same person whose body had been found at the camp site.

'We need to get the SOCO people in here to go through the place and sort out what is useful. Make a note of the name of those lawyers we will want to contact them later today. The Will in here may not be an up to date one.'

After lunch while the camp site was being searched on an inch by inch basis to see if the knife that had been used to kill Audrey Hope could be found or if there was any other piece of information laying round that could throw light on what had happened and the thorough search of her house had been carried out Thomasson sat in his office going through the various papers that had been brought back to the police station. The phone rang and the switchboard operator told him there was a Mrs Janet Davidson wanting to speak to him regarding Miss Hope.

'Inspector Thomasson speaking'
'Good afternoon Inspector my name is Janet Davidson and I am the Girl Guide County Commissioner. I expect you have been anticipating a call from me.'
'Mrs Agar did mention that she would report what had happened to you.'
'I am sorry if she was less co-operative than you could have wished but the poor woman had had a terrible experience. I quite understand the need for the police to close the site until they have been able to make the necessary searches. Quite naturally Mrs Agar we bothered about the bookings for today and the problems that their being unable to go to the site would cause.'
'I am sorry it was necessary to add to her troubles but we really had not alternative.'
'I quite understand. Its been getting those problems sorted out that has caused the delay in my contacting you. I have had a very busy morning and have had call in several favours but I have been able to find alternative locations for all the units concerned and have ensured that their units have all the information they need. So that is one thing you have no need to worry about. What I have really rung to ask you is if you have been able to identify the body. Was it one of our members?'
'I am afraid it was Mrs Davidson. The lady concerned was a Miss Audrey Hope.'
'Audrey Hope ' cried Mrs Davidson ' who could have possibly wanted to harm her. It must have been some passing lunatic.'
'Tell me Mrs Davidson do you know if Miss Hope had any relatives ?'

'I don't think she did or at least she always maintained that she had no
relations.'
'You have know her for some years I suppose ?'
'It must be fifteen years at least. My knowledge of her came entirely through
our mutual involvement in Guiding.'
'I wonder then if I might ask you to do something for me.'
'If I can.'
'As it seems there are no relatives do you think that you could make the formal
identification of the body?'
'It's the least I can do for her Inspector.'
'Thank you very much. I will send a police car to collect you and take you to
the hospital mortuary. They will then bring you here so that we can take a
formal statement.'
'There is no need to send a car. I shudder to think what my neighbours might
say if a police car arrives at my front door and I am seen being taken off in it. I
will make my own way to the hospital and then on to see you.'
'The coroner's officer will be at the hospital to facilitate things and I look
forward to seeing you later in the afternoon.'

It was about an hour later that Mrs Davidson was shown into Thomasson's
office. She was of medium height, quite slim with fair hair and grey eyes. She
was wearing a navy-blue suit that bore some badges, a blue check blouse with a
navy-blue bow tie and a blue hat. These were obviously her uniform as a Guide
Commissioner. She gave Thomasson's outstretched hand a firm shake.

'It is certainly Audrey Hope' she said ' but I still don't know how she died.'
'She was stabbed in the back with a narrow-bladed knife. One blow that pieced
her heart.'
'Then her killer was either lucky or knew exactly what they were doing.'
'Why do you say that?'
'I was a theatre sister before I married the surgeon 'Mrs Davidson smiled ' so I
know a bit about anatomy'
'Even so this must have been an unpleasant experience for you.'
'It's never easy even when you are familiar with death.'
'Then let me offer you a cup of tea.'
'Thank you that would be very welcome.'

After tea had been ordered and produced and dispensed Thomasson asked,
'What can you tell me about Miss Hope?'
'Audrey Hope was born in Fratton, Portsmouth on 17 June 1915. She attended
Portsmouth Girls Grammar School and won a place at London University where
she obtained a degree in modern languages specialising in German and Italian.

When she came down, she spent some time working in Switzerland. Indeed, she
retained a great affection for that country and visited it as often as she could.
During the war I believe she worked in a clerical capacity for the Foreign Office
using her language expertise. After the war she returned to university and
trained to be a teacher. She returned to Hampshire to teach languages at the
school she had attended as a girl. In due course she became head of department
and deputy head teacher. It was after the war that she returned to the Guide
movement, having been a Guide in her youth. She remained a leader until her
sixty fifth birthday rising to the rank of District Commissioner.'
'You certainly have a good deal of information about her 'smiled Thomasson.
'One thing about the Guide movement is that it keeps detailed records about its
members. I looked up Audrey Hope before I left home.'
'What sort of person was she? '
'I suppose she sounds somewhat old fashioned these days. She believed very
strongly in there being clear rules which everyone should follow. Discipline was
the necessary basis for personal and corporate life. If this sounds as though she
was just an old dragon you would be wrong. She was an excellent teacher and
could really get the best out of young people. She may have been demanding
but I think that looking back most of them will have appreciated what she did
for them when they were growing up. In her private life she was very strongly
anti communist. A life long member of the conservative party, indeed I think
she was on the right wing of that organisation. Whilst she did not hide her
views, she did not thrust them down anyone's throat. In some ways you might
say that she had born forty years too late. She would have made an ideal
Victorian, a mixture between class conscious observance and social service.'
'Can you think of why anyone would wish her harm?'
'Not really, I mean she was just another woman who had firm and decided
opinions about life and how it should be lived. Many of those opinions did not
sit easily with life in the last quarter of the twentieth century. She most certainly
did not agree with what she saw as the decline in standards of morality and
behaviour. But there are plenty of people of her age who hold the same points of
view.'
'There are no specific instances or events that you think could have led to what
has happened?'
'Well, there was one event that highlighted Audrey's attitude to modern youth.
She was out one day when she saw a young man hitting a young woman.
Behaviour like that was totally outside the pale to Audrey and she intervened
between them hitting the young man with her umbrella whereupon he turned on
her and knocked her to the ground. Luckily an off-duty policeman was passing
and he arrested the young man. It seems he was incensed with his girl friend
who had spent all his savings on clothes and shoes. He was found guilty of
assault and sentenced to eighteen months in prison. When he was sentenced, he
became quite violent and threatened he would deal with the interfering old

faggot when he got out. All this was at least three years ago and although I suppose he is out and about again he will have had plenty of time to cool off.'
'Do you remember his name?'
'I am afraid I don't but it should not be too difficult for the police to trace the court case.'
"And there was nothing else?'
'Not like that. Although Audrey was involved in a somewhat heated debate over the Guide Hall in Warnford. She was one of the Hall trustees. Developers wanted to buy the plot on which the Hall has stood for over sixty years to give access to other land on which they wanted to build some new homes. As an inducement they offered to provide a new plot on the edge of the village and to build new Hall with up to date facilities. Many of the locals opposed the idea. They don't want new houses with all that entails especially as the houses are likely to be beyond the reach of the local young people. Audrey, on the other hand, and quite surprisingly, given her usual conservative approach to life, was very much in favour. She saw it as a chance to train the young girls in the village as she felt they should be trained. '
'Hardly a dispute likely to lead to murder 'Thomasson observed.
'I agree except that the lead negotiator for the developers was a man called Burgess who was killed himself a week or so ago.'

After Mrs Davidson had left and Thomasson and Grant were discussing what they had learned the sergeant remarked;
'One thing is certain; I shall go up several rungs in my daughter's estimation when she hears that I have met her County Commissioner.'

CHAPTER 9

When Buxton called to see Inspector Love he felt he was as welcome as a bout of indigestion. It was clear that the Inspector liked being the big fish in the pool and did not take kindly to having his self-appointed importance challenged.

'I thought I would come and see you Inspector to bring you up to date with certain developments and to make the appropriate arrangements. You will know that there has been a second killing in the county. This time an elderly spinster who was murdered at a Girl Guide camp site. On the face of it there does not appear to be any connection with the Burgess case. However, the forensic evidence is that both people were killed in the same way and in all probability with the same weapon. Why two such different victims be killed by the same person is unclear. It is possible there is a serial killer on the loose though we have no direct evidence of this so far. However, as a result the Chief Constable has decided that the right course of action is to combine the two investigations into a single task force. He has instructed me to assume command of that task force.'

Love made no attempt to hide his disagreement.

'I find such a decision sir to be a quite unnecessary complication to what I believe to be a quite straight forward case. To my mind it was Burgess' ex girl friend who killed him. All we need to do is unlock the evidence and that means showing her so called alibi to be the fake I think it is. '
And have you been able to do that?'
'Not at the moment sir. She is a very cunning young woman but I will get her.'
'On the other hand, Inspector, you could be barking up the wrong tree.' replied Buxton.' Also, why should this young woman kill the elderly lady at a Girl Guide function?'
'With respect sir there does not seem to be any connection between the two crimes. The assumption that there is based on a doctor's view of the potential weapon.'
'Which you do not accept as it runs contrary to your theory 'retorted Buxton. 'all you seem interested in is this alibi question.'
'We have not ignored other lines of inquiry sir' Love protested 'particularly as they may assist in forming the case against the young woman.'
'Whether you agree with the decision or not Inspector, this is what is going to happen. This is what I want you to do. I want you to organise a meeting to be held here at three this afternoon. The attendees are to be yourself, your Sergeant Sparrow plus Sergeant Barnett the man who has been inspecting Burgess' books and accounts and any other officer who has been directly involved in the investigation. I am also inviting Chief Inspector Bill Underhill

of the Vice and Drugs branch to join us. You will remember that he has
information about some of the properties that Burgess owned or controlled.
Now I am going to go and have some lunch and I shall want to see all the files
you have on the case before the meeting.'
'Sir' said a disapproving Love.

After a pleasant lunch in the cathedral cloister restaurant Buxton returned to the
police station and settled down to plough through a pile of files that Sergeant
Sparrow had provided. The attendees were those that Buxton had listed to
Inspector Love plus the village constable from Upper Burford. There was also a
female constable to take notes and to produce a report on the meeting.

'I thought he may be useful sir as he knows the village better than any of us.'
Said Sparrow
'Good thinking Sergeant' Buxton nodded and noticed the scowl on Love's face.
'Good afternoon gentlemen' he said looking round the table 'and thank you for
your attendance here. The object of this meeting is to review the present state of
the investigation into the death of Nigel Burgess. Let's start with you Inspector
Love. Will you please give us the background to the case?'

Love told the meeting who Nigel Burgess was and where he lived. He then went
on to describe how his death had been reported and at what time. The described
the scene of the crime and both the original opinion of the police surgeon and
the result of the post mortem. He explained at some length his interview with
Alison Oakes and that he had formed the opinion that she had killed her former
boy friend. He finished his report by referring to the interviews that he had
conducted with some of the leading citizens of Upper Burford and the
impression he had obtained regarding the general dislike of the deceased.
However, in his view, none of this was sufficiently serious to assume that any of
the people concerned had killed the man.
 What about this alibi sergeant? 'Buxton turned to Sparrow.
'To date, sir, we have not been able to break it. Inspector Love suggested, very
wisely, that she may have taken a different route than that she said she had
followed. You will recall, sir, that she had been to Canterbury and her time of
departure was confirmed by the brewery company she had been visiting. She
claimed she had tried to telephone the deceased from a public house and we
have been able to obtain confirmation from that establishment that she did use
the phone on that day at the time she said. This obviously affects any
alternative route she may have taken. We have retraced the route she claimed to
have taken on three different days and have been unable to shake her timing. It
so happens there was a speed camera along that road on that day and if she had
tried to drive at an excessive speed, I think she would have been caught out, but

she wasn't. We have a witness as to the time she was seen coming into the village which ties in with her time of arrival.'

'We haven't exhausted all possible routes yet' pointed out Love. 'Also we are still trying to find out if anyone saw her car parked in a place that would have allowed her to walk across country, kill Burgess, get back to her car and arrive in the village at the time recorded.'

'Your motive is that she objected to being discarded by Burgess' said Chief Inspector Underhill. 'If you can't break her alibi are you arguing that she hired someone to do the killing for her?'

'I wouldn't put it beyond her ' replied Love determined to stick to his theory. 'That was going to be the next stage of the investigation.'

'We must not forget' pointed out Buxton ' that we have a second crime with what seems to be exactly the same MO. The odds must be against there being two killers especially as the stabbings seem to be the work of someone who knows how to handle a knife.'

'It may be unlikely but its not impossible' Love said.

' I know I asked the question' Underhill said 'but it doesn't mean I think its likely. I just wanted to know if it was being considered.'

'To pick up on your question Bill what do we know about this Alison Oakes Sparrow?'

'She runs her own business' said the sergeant ' a public relations consultancy based here in Chichester. She has just bought a cottage in Itchenor. To all outward appearances it's a quite successful business. We are talking to as many of the people who know her and knew Burgess and the unanimous opinion is that the break up of their relationship was by mutual consent and there were no recriminations on either side. It seems she graduated from Cambridge. The college she attended speak highly of her both as a person and a scholar. It seems she is quite musical, plays the cello and sang in the Bach choir.'

'And you are still convinced she is the guilty party Inspector ?' asked Underhill.

'She was the one who said she found the body and had the most reason for wanting revenge on Burgess for being forced to leave her life of luxury. She has to be the prime suspect Bach choir or no Bach choir.'

'Prime suspects do not always turn out to be the actual perpetrator 'Underhill said.

'What about Burgess ? 'asked Buxton ' What have we learned about him apart from the fact he had just split up with his lady friend and had managed to make himself unpopular with practically everyone in the village ? What about his business affairs Sergeant Barnett?

'There is no doubt that the business of Burgess Homes is a successful one. It is a limited company with eight branches across Sussex. Its accounting systems are first class and I have been able to satisfy myself that their client money rules are strictly observed. There is no evidence of client's money being misused. They employ a qualified accountant as their financial director and he is on top of the job. I have covered the details in my various reports sir. As well as the estate agency business the deceased also controlled a number of other companies. One of these handled the letting business offered by the estate agency. That company has the same finance director and there are clear and well documented procedures in place. The control of both these companies was in the hands of Nigel Burgess who held seventy per cent of the issued shares. The remaining thirty per cent are owned by other directors including the legal director who is a local solicitor Walter Legg. There are other directors who are simply salaried and do not hold shares. Both companies operate a well defined bonus scheme. Other companies controlled by Burgess are buy to let organisations or property development vehicles.

'And this is where we come in ' said Underhill.' You referred a schedule of properties to us to see if we knew anything about them. Can I ask why you did that?'

'It seemed an appropriate inquiry from an audit point of view sir.'

'As you know we did have knowledge of some of the properties on your list. They were being used in the sex industry but were not, as far as we knew, connected to the drug trade. You may be interested to know that we carried out one of our periodic checks on one of the properties. I chose the latest addition to the list on the grounds that we had not been there before. I was not surprised to find that all the girls who were employed in the house were foreigners but, in this case, none of them had valid identification documents. They were illegal immigrants so we took them into custody and they are in course of being repatriated. Their employers maintained that they had not realised the girls were illegals as they had recruited them through an agency. That agency turned out to be another company in the Burgess empire and by the time we called on them the people running it had scarpered. However, things got interesting when we questioned the girls. They had been recruited from their small villages and promised work as film and TV extras or models in this country. What they did not know until too late was that they were to be used as prostitutes. The usual story of sexual degradation until they were unable to refuse to do the work that was intended for them. It was do as we say or you will end up in jail. We managed to find out that they had entered the country by boat which dropped them off on some beach where a bus was waiting for them. One of the girls was brighter than the rest and made a note of the boat's name and registered port. We traced it to northern France and the French police and customs kept a watch on them. It seems they had more than one client and when they made their next trip our Customs and Excise were waiting for them. It was at that stage that it came to light that the boat was owned by a Jersey company and, surprise, surprise, that company was controlled by Nigel Burgess. Your deceased was a people smuggler and that is an industry where they take no prisoners.'

Inspector Love looked as if he had been hit by a brick but he rallied quickly and said;

'None of that invalidates the case against the girl friend.'
'Excuse me sir but there is something else I need to report 'said Sergeant Barnett.
'Go on sergeant, 'said Buxton.
'Well sir. There are some other companies to those I have already mentioned. These are property development companies. They acquire land and develop it and then sell of the properties they have built. Looking at some of these companies I noticed that they had a practice of issuing Loan Stocks when starting out on a development. These stocks were repaid in full during the course of the development. Now there is nothing outrageously strange in issuing Loan Stocks to provide a company with working capital. Often these are secured against the company's assets which will be principally the land it owns. But these were unsecured Loan Stocks and carried a very low rate of interest. When I looked closer, I was unable to find that the holders of the stock had actually contributed any funds to the company. That raised the question as to why if they had not paid for the investment, they should they be paid for its redemption. I thought it worthwhile to investigate who these so-called investors were. It was then that I discovered that they were, without exception, either senior civil servants working in the planning department of the local authority where the development land was situated or were elected members of the appropriate local authority.'
'Are you implying that these monies were bribes being paid to people who helped Burgess get the necessary approvals ?' asked Buxton
'It would appear probable sir.'
'And what have you done about this information?'
' I included it in my recent report to Inspector Love sir.'
'And what have you decided to do Inspector?' asked Buxton.
'It is a very difficult and sensitive situation sir. I am considering what is the best way forward. Some of the names supplied by the sergeant are not unknown to me. They are men of considerable local standing. This matter will require careful handling.'
'It seems to me that Sergeant Barnett may have uncovered something of considerable importance. It must be investigated without delay if only to protect those who are innocent. The people to do this are the Fraud Squad and I want Sergeant Barnett's report forwarded to them as a matter of urgency. Meanwhile I will advise the Chief Constable of the situation and also alert the Fraud Squad. See those papers go off today.'
'Yes sir.'
'Congratulations Sergeant that seems like a piece of first-class investigation. I imagine that you will be contacted by the Fraud Squad for further and fuller particulars.'
'Yes sir. Thank you, sir.'

'It looks like our Mr Burgess has been a very naughty boy one way or another'
Buxton said 'suddenly a one-horse race has attracted quite a field of runners.'
'Whoever topped him seems to have done us a good turn' grinned Underhill.
'With respect gentlemen 'Love said 'whilst this new information is very
interesting it does not move us forward in discovering who did kill the man. In
my experience the first idea is often the best one.'
'But you are no further forward in proving it was the girl friend than you were
the day the body was discovered' snorted Underhill. 'In my book you have to be
careful when dealing with an idée fixe.'
'What we need to do 'said Buxton firmly' is decide on our next steps. Bill, can
your people try and find if there are any stirrings in the undergrowth that might
show if someone had a score to settle with Burgess?'
'Will do Richard.'
'Love, you are going to send Barnett's report to the Fraud Squad and the Chief
will decide how we are going to follow up on it. In the meanwhile, I want you
contact all the people with whom Burgess had business contacts and, by general
enquiries, find out what they knew of him and see if any of them have any
information they are willing to pass on. Make it sound like a routine enquiry
and see what sort of alibi they produce for the evening in question. Constable
Watson have you picked up anything interesting around the village?
'Nothing special sir' replied Watson 'just the usual gossip and speculation. One
or two of the men have been shooting their mouths off in The Red Bull but it
was clear they didn't really know anything. I had a quiet word with a couple of
them. Pointed out the people they were talking about most likely had lawyers
and if they didn't want to be on the receiving end of a solicitor's letter, they had
better watch what they were saying.'
'Well done Watson' laughed Buxton 'but I want you to continue to keep your
ears and eyes open in the village just in case something crops up that might
throw some light on what happened. 'As you have already found people are
more likely to talk loosely in the pub. Keep Inspector Love informed of
anything you hear that could be of interest.'
'Very good sir.'
'Two people we are going to need to speak to are Burgess' lawyer and his
accountant. I want to know how much they knew of their client's business
affairs. Barnett, do you know the name of Burgess' accountant?'
'I know who the auditors are for his companies but I have not been into his
personal finances. As far as I can see few of his companies paid any dividends.
They retained their profits for future investment. I am planning to talk to all the
auditors.'
'Keep us posted on what you find out 'said Buxton 'Where are we with his
personal finances Love?'
'That information should be in his papers Sparrow.'
'I will let you have a report on that in a couple of days sir' said Sparrow

'What about his bank? 'asked Buxton
'The usual cagey answer sir. Nothing beyond confirming he was a customer.'
'Tell me which bank it is and leave that one with me. By the way was the house registered in his name?'
'There was a separate company for that 'said Barnett 'all the shares bar one in the name of Walter Legg were held by Burgess who seems to have provided the working capital.'

Driving home Buxton found himself reviewing what they knew about Nigel Burgess. It was plain he was an out and out crook but his sudden death had allowed him no time to cover his tracks. He would never have assumed that anyone would take an in depth look into his activities. The Customs and Excise and the unit who specialised in people smugglers would deal with that side of things. With Burgess dead there was little they could do about him but they might uncover some useful leads. The question of the bribing of local government officers and elected councillors would be handled by the Fraud Squad. What was needed was to try and find out if anyone connected with those activities had decided that Burgess was a danger or an unwelcome rival and had to be removed. He doubted if the bribery cases would produce anyone but they had to be sure. The people smugglers were a different kettle of fish. You could not rule out that activity being the cause of his death. Also, he should not overlook the chance, remote as it may seem, that there was a random killer on the loose. If there was then it was likely there would be another case before long. If there wasn't a random killer then why had these two very different people been killed by what appeared to be the same hand. One thing was clear. They were nowhere near the end of the road.

As he neared home, he gave a sigh. He still had not got used to the idea that his wife would not be waiting for him and that he would be going back to an empty flat. Not only that but he would have to look after himself, there would be no cooked meal or welcoming drink. Brighton was not short of good restaurants and he could always be sure of finding a satisfactory dinner. Even so, he would have to dine on his own and return to an empty flat. His had been a happy marriage and he wondered how long it would take to get used to the fact he had lost Doreen forever.

CHAPTER 10

Richard Buxton was reading through the latest reports on the Burgess case when his phone buzzed.

'Buxton speaking'
'Good morning sir' came the polite female voice ' the AC would be grateful if you could spare him a few moments.'
'I'll be along in a couple of shakes ' he replied. As he made his way to the top floor he wondered if the Chief had had another letter from Mrs Trumper. This time complaining about him.
'Good morning Richard. Take a pew. Have you had a chance to read the reports on this case at the Girl Guide Campsite?'
'Yes sir. The body has been identified and her property searched. They are processing the papers they have found and have made a start on contacting the eighty odd people who were at the event on the night of the killing.'
'The Chief is more than a bit concerned about this case Richard.'
'Why is that sir. It's very early days yet and I think Thomasson, the inspector in charge is no-one's fool'
'It's not that which is bothering him. It seems that his wife is about to become the Regional President of this FG2 organisation. You've met Lady Mary haven't you ?'
'On one occasion sir.'
'Then you will know that she has a definite personality if I can put it that way. She appears to have issued a domestic edict that this case is to be solved with the minimum of delay and without bringing the name of Guiding into disrepute. The Chief, anxious I suspect to maintain domestic harmony, has decided that you should personally take charge of the case. That way he can tell Lady Mary that he has put his most senior officer on the job. Sorry to add to your burdens but there it is.'
'A case of she who must be obeyed sir' grinned Buxton.
'Exactly. Please let the Chief have daily reports on progress. I have a nasty feeling this isn't going to be a simple one to solve.'
'Let's hope you are wrong sir.'

Driving over to the police headquarters in Horsham Buxton mulled over how best to break the news to Thomasson. He could understand that the younger man would not be pleased to find he had been relieved of control of what was likely to be his first big murder inquiry when he had only been on the job for one day. Buxton knew that had he been in that position he would have been furious. But neither of them had any option. Shown into Thomasson's office he could see the questions in the other man's eyes. After some general conversation he asked,

'Have you had the post mortem report on Audrey Hope? If so what did it say?'
'She was killed by a single blow in the back with a thin bladed knife. The knife went straight into the left ventricle. Death was instantaneous. The killer either had a knowledge of anatomy or was lucky.'
'Interesting 'said Buxton. 'Tell me how well acquainted are you with the Burgess case in Upper Burford? '
'I know of it sir but have no detailed information.'
'Then you will be interested to know that Burgess was killed by a single knife blow in the back with a narrow-bladed knife that penetrated the left ventricle.'
'Was he by heck 'exclaimed Thomasson 'coincidence or connection. What's your feeling sir?'
'I am not a great believer in coincidences.' replied Buxton and looked at his watch although he was well aware of the time. 'It's lunch time. If you are free let's go and get something to eat. I take it you know of a decent pub in these parts.'

Over a chicken curry and a pint of lager Buxton revealed the true reason for his visit.

'Audrey Hope had attended a function organised by the FG2 group. It so happens that the Chief Constable's wife is about to become the Regional President of this organisation. I don't know if you have ever met Lady Mary but she is a formidable personality and she is not enamoured of the idea of being head of a body where one of its members is subject to an unsolved murder. Hence the Chief has issued a directive that I am to assume responsibility for the inquiry. This should buy him some domestic peace. I am sorry to usurp your position Thomasson but I have no option. I know that if I were in your place I would not be a happy bunny. So, let me assure you that I see this as a combined operation. If there is any glory to come out of it, I shall see you get your fair share. If there is only grief then I will take the hit. In any event I think we are going to have to combine the two investigations. Although I have read your report, I want you to talk me through what happened and what steps you have taken so that I can get up to speed on what is happening and what needs to be done. I think it might be a good idea to have your sergeant in on this as well as I gather he is dealing with finding out the names of the people who were there that night which, in itself, is going to be a deal of work trying to find who was where and who saw or heard what.'

Back at the station Buxton, Thomasson and Grant reviewed all that had happened right from the time the first phone call was received right through to the visit from Mrs Davidson. Grant told them how he had arranged for the FG2 County Secretary to provide the name, address and phone number of the secretary to each of the individual groups whose members would have been at the function. He had passed this information to the local police and asked them to obtain the names of their members who had been at the Camp Fire. When they had that information, they were to question each individual and get full information as to how they got to the site, what they did during the evening, who they were with throughout that time and who they saw or spoke to. Had they noticed anyone acting strangely, anyone who did not appear to be a member of FG2 or had they heard any strange noises. The information received from these interviews would be collated and cross checked for accuracy and confirmation. It would take some days for this work to be done. Thomasson reported that the search of the camp site had not produced anything that could be seen as being useful and there seemed little point in not allowing the site, apart from the chapel area, to re-open.

'You mentioned that Mrs Agar closed the gate when she thought everyone had left. Did she not check the car park? 'asked Buxton
'The car park was in the dark and there were no lights coming from it she assumed it was empty. She says she was very tired and had a busy day ahead of her tomorrow so went to bed.'
'Any luck with the young man who knocked her over?' he asked Grant.
'I got his name from records just before you came in sir' he replied. 'he is called Norman Vale. The outside caterers are a firm called Mobile Meals based in Crawley. My next job is to contact them and get confirmation that Vale was part of their workforce at the camp site. If he was then I want his address. Then we can see what he has to say for himself'
'Right,' said Buxton 'then you Grant get on with the collating of the evidence from those who were at this bean feast. I think it would also be a good idea if you questioned Vale.'
'Thomasson I would like you to go to Warnford and find out what you can about the proposals for the Guide Hall. Try and find out how deep are the divisions over the idea of accepting the offer that's been made.'
'Very good sir.'
'Mrs Davidson has given you a lot of useful background. I take it all this has been included in her statement.'
'Yes sir, 'confirmed Grant.
'We need to find out what her papers reveal about the lady and contact her lawyer to see if she had changed her Will. If she had not, I see no reason why you should not open the envelope containing the copy and read it. This is a case where I think its going to be most important to find out as much as we can about the victim to see if we can discover what it was that drove someone to kill her.'

At this point there was a knock at the door and a uniformed constable entered.

'Excuse me sir but we have a gentleman at the counter asking to speak to someone about Miss Hope. He says he is the secretary of the Conservative Association.'
'You had better show him in constable. You have more than enough to get on with sergeant so we won't keep you from your work.'
'Thank you, sir,' Grant replied and left with a folder of papers under his arm.

He was followed shortly after by the constable opening the door and announcing

'Mr Franklin sir' and closed the door behind the newcomer who was a man in his seventies with short grey hair, blue eyes and a small moustache. His complexion was ruddy and his face round with a somewhat bulbous nose. He wore a navy-blue blazer, a checked shirt with a military looking tie, twill trousers and brightly polished brown brogue shoes.

'Chief Superintendent Buxton' he stood and held out a hand. 'And you are sir ?'
'Frederick Ball, retired colonel of the Royal Artillery.'
'This is Inspector Thomasson colonel. How can we be of assistance to you? Please take a seat.'
'I have called in reference to a Miss Audrey Hope. I have been given to understand she has met with a fatal accident. Is that true? There is certainly no-one at her home and a neighbour told me the police had been at the house.'
'I am sorry to have to tell you sir that Miss Hope was killed the night before last.'
'Killed ! Do you actually mean murdered?'
'Yes sir.'
'Good grief! What is the world coming to? Who did it? Some passing young thug I suppose. We are far too soft on these people. Bring back capital punishment is what I say.'
'At the moment we have no idea who was responsible. Miss Hope was attending a Guide function at a camp site when she was struck down.'
'Some passing thug mark my words Superintendent.'
'Can I ask you why you were asking about Miss Hope colonel?'
'Yes, of course, must state my business. The thing is I am the secretary of the Mid Weald Conservative Association and Miss Hope was our treasurer. I am going to need to obtain the papers that were in her possession relating to her role as treasurer and to make alternative banking arrangements. I presume that the police have taken control of her house and I need to get those papers.'
'I quite understand colonel. I wonder inspector if you would check with Sergeant Grant as to whether the papers that the colonel is wanting is among those collected from the house?'
'Yes, of course, replied Thomasson and left the room.

'I suppose you knew Miss Hope quite well colonel?'
'Known her for getting on for twenty years. A first class person absolutely first class.'
'What can you tell me about her colonel? In instances like this it is important that we learn as much as is possible about the victim'
'Miss Hope was a school teacher and, from what I hear, a first class one. One of the old school you know. Believed in discipline and hard work. Had no time for all these long-haired idiots with their fancy ideas about allowing children to develop as they wished. School children like an army battalion need a strict command basis and unquestioning obedience. She had no time with these bureaucrats in Brussels. Saw our being a member of the Common Market as nothing short of a surrender to foreigners. Had nothing but contempt for these left-wing idiots that rule the socialists these days nor for their communist sympathisers.'
'Do you have any idea what she did before she became a teacher colonel ?'
'Once she mentioned that she had worked in Switzerland as a young woman. She admired them and their country. Went there as often as she could. During the war years she was employed in a government office I gather in a secretarial role. Became a teacher at the end of the war. Been a member of the party eve since nineteen forty-five. Joined in protest against Atlee and his band of thieves.'

At this point Inspector Thomasson returned with some a bundle of papers.

'Here you are colonel. One folder entitled Conservative Association, a cheque book, a paying in book, some bank statements and a cash book. Are these what you are looking for?'
'Seems like it 'the colonel looked at the papers and the cash book. 'Yes, this is what I need.'
'Then perhaps you would be good enough to sign this receipt for them. We will have to provide her solicitor with a receipt for everything we have taken from the house so your receipt will clarify what has happened to these papers.'
 The colonel signed the receipt and with a blunt wish, which was as near an order as he could make it, said he hoped that they would catch the killer without delay and went on his way.

'What did you make of him sir? Thomasson asked having shown the colonel to the exit.
'Colonel Blimp is alive and well 'grinned Buxton. 'He has underlined what Mrs Davidson told you. Audrey Hope was a school marm of the old type. Rules are rules and you had better obey them. School, like life, should have a strict hierarchy and everyone should know their place. Her politics, as if they were important, were very right wing. Oh, and he confirmed that she worked as a

secretary for some government ministry during the war. Before that she had
been in Switzerland. She liked the country and admired the people. See if you
can get anything more about her from her neighbours, any friends she may have
had and her former colleagues in the school and the Guides. You never know
something might crop up that will indicate why someone wanted to stick a knife
in her back.'

The next morning Buxton had a long talk with the Assistant Commissioner.
They agreed that all the indications were that the two killings were connected in
that they had been carried out by the same hand. It made sense therefore to
combine the two investigations because it was always possible that something
learned about one crime could link into something connected with the other
crime. As the Chief Constable had ordered, Buxton to lead the Audrey Hope
case and as he had involved in him in the Burgess case to protect himself from a
troublesome lady the obvious thing was for Buxton to head up the combined
investigation.

'By the way Richard the media are on to both these crimes. You will have to
make a statement to them today at eleven fifteen. I don't need to tell you that we
want to keep them friendly without giving away anything vital. Just the usual
thing, inquiries are continuing and if anyone has any information will they
please let us know. I should start with just the Hope case and wait and see if
they try to link it to the Burgess case. If they do be helpful but uninformative.
The last thing we want is to give the killer the idea we are on to him.'
'Very good sir'

At the appointed hour Buxton exited the building and spoke to a small crowd of
journalists and TV news programmes. He confirmed the death of Audrey Hope
and spoke about the event that had taken place that evening. He pointed out that
their inquiries were at an early stage and asked that anyone who had any
information contact the police. The questions were routine ones. Had anyone
else been injured? No. Did he think that the security at the camp site had been
at fault? He did not think so in all the circumstances. Had the next of kin been
informed? They had been unable to trace any next of kin. Did he think this was
a random killing? He repeated that it was early days to make such an assertion.
Just when he thought he was going to get away easily came the question about
the Burgess case? Did the police think there was any connection? Yes, there
were two deaths from stabbing but that did not necessarily imply a connection.
When pressed he said the police were interested in facts not speculations and
brought the conference to an end.

'Thank God that's over 'he said to Thomasson who had joined him.

CHAPTER 11

Having uncovered Nigel Burgess' involvement in the sex industry and in people smuggling Chief Inspector Bill Underhill took a close interest in the follow up investigations. A first step was to raid the other properties owned by a Burgess company where it was known that it was used as a massage parlour. In each case he found that the young women working in them were illegal immigrants even though some of them produced what they claimed to be valid passports. The tenants of the properties were charged with running immoral properties and the girls were scheduled for deportation although, inevitably, they appealed and that process took a long time during which some of the girls slipped off the radar. The properties were closed down and the landlord, now the executors of the Burgess estate took the opportunity to foreclose on the grounds of non payment of rent. The people who had run the houses were usually middle-aged women.

Maude Pontin was in her fifties but, with thick makeup and a short skirt to add to the dyed blonde hair tried to look about thirty-five. Underhill told her their interview was to be taped.

'You have nothing against me 'was her opening gambit when questioned by Underhill. 'I was simply doing a job of work. I was paid a wage and all the rest of the money was paid over to the company that owned the house.'
'You say that you were just doing a job of work. But it's a fact isn't it that the lease of the property was in your name. That puts you right in the firing line. Legally you are the one who is operating a property for immoral purposes.'
'I tell you it wasn't my business. I was hired to do a job of work that's all there was to it.'
'You say all the money other than your wages went to the owner.
'That's right.'
'Then how is it that the rates, the electricity and the water are all in your name?' asked Underhill.
'That was just for convenience.'
'You said that all the money apart from your salary went to the owner.'
'That's right.'
'Then where did the money to pay the girls and all those bills come from ?'
'Come on, use your nut ' snorted Maude ' what I meant was after all the costs had been paid.'
'Then why didn't you say so.?'
'Because I am not a bloody accountant.'
'Your customers paid cash?'
'Of course. You don't think we took credit cards or cheques do you.'
'How did you pay over the profits?'

'I put them in an envelope and sent it off registered post to an address in Portslade.'
'What was that address?'
'That's for you to find out.'
'Look Maude this isn't some small time misdemeanour. There is a killing involved.'
'A killing ! Now look here copper you can't lay that on to me. Who has been topped?'
'The man who owned the property. So, you see Maude there was a lot of money at stake. It could well have paid someone to have him put out of the way. Where were you on the early evening of April 25th ?'
'I was working. You can ask any of the girls.'
'I ask again, what was the address to which you sent your registered letters and who were they addressed to?'
'Hang on a moment ' Maude opened her handbag and produced a business card which she threw across the desk. 'Pick the bones out of that.'
Underhill put the card in his file before asking;
'Who else knew about these arrangements?'
'No-one. I got my instructions when I signed the lease and was told in no uncertain terms to keep my mouth shut.'
'Who by?'
'He didn't give his autograph.'
'Did any of the girls ever do a runner?'
'It's been known.'
'What happened then?'
'I put in a note with the money. '
'And?'
'I got a message through the door telling when a new girl would arrive.'
'How much did you know about how these girls came to be in this country?'
'Nothing. One thing I learned a long time ago was not to ask questions. Not if you wanted to stay healthy.'
'What do you mean 'stay healthy' ?'
'Some people don't take kindly to having others nosing into their affairs. They can turn nasty if you do. After all I wasn't running a Sunday School '
 Underhill pressed a button on the desk and said;
'This interview is terminated. '
 When a constable entered he said
'Send her back to the remand centre '
 'Bloody coppers' snarled Maude as she was led away.

This interview was much the same as those with the other women who ran these houses for Burgess. Further enquiries showed that all the women were on duty six evenings a week just having Sunday off. None of them had killed Burgess.

This led to the people smuggling activities. The crew of the boat claimed that they knew nothing about anything apart from the fact that they received instructions to pick up a cargo at a named port in France or Belgium and deliver it to a given spot off the coast of Kent or Sussex or occasionally Norfolk. There the boat would be met by a dinghy, the cargo offloaded, and they returned to their home port. When asked how they got their instructions they said there would be a message in the personal column of a Jersey paper that meant that they were to go to a certain address to pick up an envelope. This envelope contained their instructions. When asked how they were paid they said that the money came through from an international money transfer company and they collected it on the last working day of each month. In between voyages they were free to go fishing and sell what they caught. The day Burgess was killed they were in Ostend waiting for a cargo and this was shown to be correct. In any event they had never heard of Nigel Burgess and so had no idea where he lived.

The company in whose name the boat was registered at a foreign bank with an office in St Helier. They provided a company management service providing two directors, being one of their local managers and the wife of the manager of their branch in Sark. All they knew was that the boat was an investment held by Nigel Burgess who kept it for personal use. The present manager could not recall ever meeting his customer, all contact had been carried out by post with the accommodation address in Portslade.

One piece of information that had surfaced was that Burgess supplied women not only for his own properties but for others in the same business. By checking the boat's log, they were able to obtain some dates and asked police forces round the country if any of them had information about the use of illegal immigrants in local massage parlours. If so were there any rumours about girls arriving at the dates supplied? This produced positive responses from Birmingham, Leicester and Oxford. When parlours in these places were raided and those running them questioned none of them admitted to knowing a Nigel Burgess despite the fact that the questioning of the girls identified nearly ten occasions when their arrival coincided with the dates in the fishing boat's log. The parlour owners were traced and whilst they had to concede they had business dealings with a Burgess company none of them had ever met him or knew where he lived added to which each of them provided a solid alibi for the day of his death.

CHAPTER 12

It had been agreed that Inspector Thomasson visit Warnford to try and get a better understanding of the situation regarding the Guide Hall. Mrs Davidson had told him that the local rector was the chairman of the Hall trustees but before he called at the Rectory he decided to have a look at the Hall itself to get an idea of the layout. He found it near the centre of the village street; it was a wooden building which looked more like a cricket pavilion than a meeting place. Opening the double gates, he followed a path that was made up and wide enough to take a car and which led to a small parking space. There were double doors at the front of the building with shutters and there were two locks on the door. Walking round the building he saw that there were shuttered windows on both sides but not at the back. Behind the Hall was a quite large area of grass in the centre of which was a flagpole. At the far end of the grounds there was a surprisingly big rockery covered in shrubs and plants that seemed to have been built to afford a barrier to the farmland behind the Hall plot. Thomasson guessed the building must be decades old by the nature of its construction and the almost black stained wooden walls. He could understand that the prospect of a new building would have its attractions to the current users.

Returning to the road he made for the readily observable church tower where he expected to find the Rectory. Sure enough there was a large Victorian house next to the church but the sign on its gate
said 'Old Rectory'. The Church Commissioners had clearly decided t capitalise on the big house and provide a newer and more modern residence for the Rector. He turned into the churchyard and up the drive to the south door which led into a porch with the two walls covered in a variety of posters and notices. He quickly picked up the one which gave the name of the Rector as the Reverend Peter Coventry and his address as The Rectory, School Lane, Warnford. He was about to leave the church in search of the Rectory when the inner door opened and a clergyman appeared. He was a tall man in his forties with short brown hair going grey at the temples and horned rimmed glasses. He was carrying a number of heavy looking books.

'Can I help you?' he asked.
'Reverend Coventry?'
'That's me' he said with a nod of his head.

Thomasson introduced himself.

'I don't think I have ever had a visit from a policeman'
' I am investigating the death of Miss Audrey Hope'
'Ah yes, a most sad event. Perhaps you had better come into the vestry.'

He led the way down a side aisle of the ancient church and unlocked a door that led into a small office.

'Take a seat Inspector and tell me how I can help.'

'I am told that you are chairman of the trustees of the Guide Hall sir.'

'Yes that is one of a whole range of burdens that I found were laid upon the Rector when I came to this benefice. It seems that the local incumbent has held the Chairman's slot ex-officio ever since the Hall was built over sixty years ago.'

'Miss Hope was also a trustee I understand.'

'That is correct. She was the representative named by the Guide County Commissioner. An appointment that is covered in the Hall constitution. But why all this interest in our Guide Hall?'

'I am also told that the future of the Hall is under discussion sir.'

'Yes, an offer has been made to acquire the site so that it can be used as access to the land at the rear which is scheduled for housing development. The purchaser has offered another plot of land plus the construction of a brick building with modern facilities as an inducement.'

'Has that offer been accepted?'

' Not at the moment. This is a conservative village Inspector and many of its residents do not welcome change, especially if that change involves newcomers arriving.'

'Can you tell me what Miss Hope's view was ?'

'She was very much in favour of the proposal which may seem a little strange given her general philosophy. In her view the new Hall would allow its use for a whole range of activities from play groups to pack holidays for Brownies.'

'Was her view that of the majority sir?'

'No. The trustees seem equally divided which puts me in an awkward position. Whichever way I decide its likely to be unpopular with some folk. Quite frankly Inspector it's a problem I could well do without. I have not been here long; previously I was chaplain at St. Barnolph's college in Oxford. Unfortunately, I suffered health problems and had to resign that position. I came to Sussex hoping for a less stressful parish where I could find space to follow my theological research only to find myself in the middle of disputing factions which is not the position a rector should be in. Between you and me I am in touch with the County Commissioner with a view to my retiring from the trusteeship. The building is a Girl Guide Association property and, in my opinion, they should appoint the chairman of the trustees from their own organisation. The notion that the Rector should fill this kind of role is out dated.''

'Do you think it possible that someone who disagreed with Miss Hope could have taken extreme action to stop her winning the debate?'

'What a dreadful idea Inspector. I most sincerely hope and pray that is not the case.'

'Yet the man who led the purchase proposal was himself killed a couple of weeks ago.'
'Do you mean Mr Nigel Burgess?'
'Yes sir.'
'But that is terrible news. I did not know the man well nor did I find him a particularly pleasant person, but you cannot be suggesting that both he and Miss Hope were killed for the same reason?'
'That is what we are trying to find out Mr Coventry. One of the important things in an investigation such as this is to get to understand the victim. How would you describe Miss Hope sir?'
'I do not claim to have known her that well Inspector. From what I knew, which was solely in connection with her membership of the Guide Hall committee, she was, I would say, a traditionalist. She preferred the familiar ways and she certainly did not approve of many of the modern traits in our society. Some of her ideas appeared to be outdated to be frank. I think she rather harked back to the old days when people were supposed to know their place and where society had a clearly defined structure. She found it difficult to accept modern ideas such as the greater place in public life being played by women. In her book it was the duty of those in authority to set the rules and of those not in authority to obey them without too many questions. She was something of an anachronism. I really think she regretted the days when Britain ruled a quarter of the planet. '
'In other words not the easiest person get along with.'
'Maybe not Inspector but there is a great deal of difference between disliking a person and killing them.'

The County Commissioner had given Thomasson the names and addresses of the other trustees and he spent the rest of the morning visiting them and asking them about the proposal for the Guide Hall and their recollection of Audrey Hope as a woman. He also verified that none of them had been at the event at the camp site. They were what may be called village worthies with no direct involvement in the guiding movement.

The first person he spoke to was a Mrs Victor who was the wife of the local vet. She was not in favour of the proposal on the grounds that the village did not have the infrastructure to take an additional fifty houses. When asked about Miss Hope's view she said that although that lady was very much a traditionalist in most matters she was very forward looking when it came to facilities for young people. In her book a good building would attract more girls and this itself would open the way for them to be properly trained into becoming worthwhile adults. The next on the list was a Mr. Cyril Orchard who was a retired bank manager and financial adviser to the other trustees. He was in agreement with Miss Hope on the grounds that the offer was a financially attractive one which would offer a solution to the ongoing problem of maintaining the present hall in a good state of repair and in line with ever increasing legal requirements. He really knew very little about Miss Hope as a person but found her contributions to the trustees' meetings to have been soundly based. Lastly, Thomasson spoke to a Captain Graham Long who expressed himself as strongly opposed to the proposal on the grounds that the village was as big as was necessary and there was no reason why it should welcome incomers who would probably contribute little or nothing to the social life of the village as they were likely to be commuters from Portsmouth or Brighton. He did not claim to know Miss Hope well but found her, and her ideas, were soundly based.

Coming away from these meetings Thomasson found himself feeling sympathy with the Reverend Coventry who was in the middle of what could well prove to be a divisive debate.   He decided to have some lunch and then to drive into Portsmouth and visit the school where Audrey Hope had taught for so many years.

'I hope this visit does not mean that one of our pupils is in trouble with the law Inspector' the headmaster said when he had ushered Thomasson to a seat in his book lined study.
'Not to my knowledge Mr. Westwood' Thomasson smiled. He looked across at the man who sat behind the desk. He had fairly long grey hair, brown eyes and the rather tired look of a   man who was finding life a far from easy road. He was, Thomasson guessed approaching retirement age.
'Then how can I be of assistance to you?'
'I have called in connection with our investigation into the death of Miss Audrey Hope who was, I understand, a teacher at this school for a good many years.'
'I had heard of course about Audrey's death and have to admit it came as a considerable shock to me.'
'Can you tell me how long she was on the staff of the school?'
'I can because, when I heard what had happened to her, I started on a bit of research as there will have to be a reference to her in the next school magazine. She came to the school originally in 1949 straight after she had finished at London University. She had been to school in the city as a young girl and wanted to return to her roots. She came to teach modern languages primarily French and German although in later years we added Italian and Spanish to the options for our pupils though we employed specialist teachers for those languages. She was a little older than most newly qualified teachers as she had not entered the profession until after the war.'
'Do you know what she did during the war sir?'

'From what she said, which was never a great deal, she worked in a clerical position for a government department.'

'Do you happen to know which one Mr Westwood?'

'Now you mention it I don't think she ever said which department it was. Anyway, she settled into teaching and stayed at the school until she retired some five years ago.'

'I assume she attained some seniority during that time.'

'She did indeed. She was for many years the head of department and for the last five years she was here she was deputy head mistress.'

'May I ask what sort of teacher she was?'

'A rather odd question Inspector.'

'Not really sir, you see in cases such as this it is important that we get to know as much as we can about the deceased. It's often only by understanding the victim that we are able to find the killer.'

'An interesting point of view Inspector' the headmaster replied as he appeared to consider and digest it 'Yes, you asked about her as a teacher. In fact, she was a very successful one if you consider her in the terms of the results obtained by her pupils. She was a strict disciplinarian who expected high standards of work and behaviour from her pupils. That may seem to argue against her obtaining good results but, in fact, for some strange reason her pupils respected her and were prepared to work hard for her. I think it possibly came down to their feeling innately comfortable to be in a defined environment.'

'As you probably know she was also a Girl Guide leader sir.'

'So she was and I suspect she ran her units like she ran her classes.'

'Did she lead any school trips to other countries sir?'

'Yes, it was very much part of her belief that the best way to interest young people in a language is to expose them to the country where it is spoken. To know and understand how the locals lived and the nature of their society was, in her view, an essential part of learning a language.'

'Which countries did she visit?'

'Germany and Switzerland were her choice of countries. In the early years it was not easy to go to Germany but once the reconstruction was complete, she added it to the list.'

'I presume she went to different parts in different years to give some variety.'

'Not at all she was quite regular in her choice of destinations. By far her favourite was Zurich which is German speaking. She had worked in Switzerland I believe before the war and was attracted by the scenery and the people.'

'What about her relationships with other members of the staff?'

'Audrey was not the easiest of people to get on with. She had very fixed ideas. In fact, she was, to be quite frank, old fashioned. I think she believed that when Britain lost its empire it was as big a tragedy as when Rome lost its empire. She tended to view modern Britain as though it was as it must have been after the Romans left. Added to that her social views were more akin to those of a latter-day Victorian than to a second half of the twentieth century woman. Nothing wrong in that and she most certainly did not let it adversely affect her teaching. After all her subject was languages not social sciences. You asked how she got along with her colleagues. The answer to that is that provided she felt that the proper standards were being maintained she took her part in the staff room community.   As the years went by the younger members of staff found her something of a dinosaur but generally accepted her for what she was a really successful teacher. The only trouble area was politics. Audrey was a right-wing Tory, she was very vocal at the time of the Common Market Referendum in the early seventies, while some of the young people were very much on the left wing in their views. There were some quite heated exchanges at one time which led to my issuing an edict that politics and religion were not to be discussed in the staff room.'

'Which leads me to ask sir if you know of anyone who might have wished her harm? '

'I do not think anyone took these disputes that seriously. Besides she has been retired for five years. If anyone was going to do anything, they would have done it long before now.'

'Is there any teacher on the staff now who you feel it might be useful for me to talk to sir?'

The headmaster thought for a moment and then said;

'The best person to talk to would be Tom Martin. He is our head of history and geography and has been at the school for over twenty years. Let me see, 'he opened a folder and studied it 'yes, Tom is free now and will be in the staff room. I will go and ask him to come along here. You can talk in private in this room and I will do a tour of the school. It doesn't do any harm to any of them to see the 'Old Man' prowling about.' He added with a laugh.

The man who came into the room was in his late fifties, sturdily built with short grey hair and a goatee beard. He was wearing a tweed jacket with leather patches on the elbows, baggy brown trousers and suede boots.'

'Tom Martin' he held out a hand and had a surprisingly firm grip.

'Inspector Thomasson of the Sussex Police. Thank you for sparing the time to talk to me. Has the headmaster explained the reason for my visit?'

'No, he just said that a policeman wished to talk to me. That kind of statement amuses him. May I ask what this about?'

'Of course. It is in connection with the death of Miss Audrey Hope.'

'She's been retired for years why come and ask questions here?'

' It's important that we learn as much as possible about the deceased in a case such as this.'

'To be frank I had thought, from what I had read and heard that it must be a random attack. I realise Audrey had her own ideas on education and society but I should doubt if they were to cause anyone to take such drastic action.'

'You worked with her for a number of years I believe Mr Martin?'

'Yes, it must have been, I don't know, getting on for fifteen years but we were in different departments and had no close scholastic connections. We had no social contacts in common so I can't claim to have known her that well.'

'How would you sum her up as a fellow member of staff?'

'She was an excellent teacher. All you need do to confirm that is examine the exam results of her students. As a person I have to admit that we had little or nothing in common. Time brings change with it Inspector and some people find it hard if not impossible to adjust to those changes. Audrey Hope was one of them. Her views remained firmly based in the social structure and behaviour of the eighteen nineties. She believed that this country had a God given right to rule over as many people as it chose. That and the superiority of the British navy were her foundations. When both of these pillars collapsed before her eyes, she found it hard to reconcile herself to life in the second half of the twentieth century. The best way to handle Audrey was with a long spoon' he laughed. 'By that I mean avoid any topic that might bring out the Rule Britannia in her. '

'Did everyone have your laid-back approach Mr Martin?'

'Not at all. As the years went by and we had young people, newly out of university, joining the staff, people from very different social backgrounds to Audrey, there was some friction.'

'Can you think of anyone who took serious exception to her views?'

'There was one young man called Grant Cooper who came to us to teach junior science. He was as far left wing as Audrey was in the other direction. He was a rather scrawny individual with untidy sandy hair and he wore rimless glasses and always looked as if he had been pulled through a hedge backwards. Having said that he was, I understand a brilliant physicist but a useless teacher. He and Audrey did not mix well. Many of us got sick and tired of those two going hammer and tongs and complained to the Head who issued an edict that politics and religion were banned from the staff room. If there was one type of person that was anathema to Audrey it was a communist. Talk about a red rag to a bull' he chuckled.

'What happened sir?'

'Oh, Copper did not stay long. He stood for the local council and got under a hundred votes. He even stood for parliament and got under two hundred votes and lost his deposit. The party he stood for, well you could hardly call it a party, was the APR.'

'I can't recall ever hearing of it.'

'I am not surprised. It was the Army of the Proletariat Republic. The last two words sum up its policies. As for being an army I doubt if they could muster a platoon. Anyway, he left after the general election for a post in Liverpool where the politics were more in tune with his. One thing I do remember about him was that I was present at the declaration of the poll at the general election. I was supporting the Liberal candidate. Audrey was also there supporting the Tory candidate who won with an impressive majority. As the whole thing was breaking up I heard Cooper say to Audrey something along the lines that she may have won this skirmish but the Army would win the war and the gutters would run with blood of people like her. He had been drinking. Probably to drown his sorrows but he was not exactly sober when he said that. I will say this for Audrey she laughed in his face, turned her back on him and walked away.'

'So he actually threatened her did he Mr Martin?'

'More like hot air than an actual threat in my view. The man was a paper tiger if ever there was one.'

'Thank you for your assistance sir. I should be most grateful if you could call at the police station when convenient and get what you have told me down into a formal statement. '

'If you wish but I doubt if it will serve any useful purpose.'

When Thomasson got back to his office, he found Sergeant Grant waiting for him.

'The search people found this file' he laid a buff folder on the desk' under some paper in a drawer in the spare room. 'In view of what people have told us about the deceased I thought you might find it interesting sir.'

Thomasson opened the folder and found it contained a dozen or so leaflets issued by the Army of the Proletarian Republic. They set out the Army policies and how they proposed to put them into effect when the people had risen up against the monarchy and the existing social order.

'Not the kind of thing I should have thought was to Miss Hope's taste.'

Thomasson looked at them and noted that each one had an addressed label attached to it and the address was that of Miss Audrey Hope.

'Ever heard of these people, sir ?' asked Grant.

'Not until this afternoon. Take a seat and I will tell you a story.'

'Did you hear the news this morning?' Trevor Nightingale asked as he sipped his half pint of best bitter.

'Local or national?' asked Olga Sanderson.

'Local'

'No, we didn't. Was there something interesting that we missed?'

'Only that there has been another murder.?

'What here in the village' squeaked Olivia.

'Not here. It was on Friday night and took place in a Girl Guide Camp Site over near Horsham.'

'It wasn't a young girl was it?' asked Olga.

'No, it was an elderly woman' said Trevor.

'They are not enrolling pensioners as Girl Guides now are they' giggled Olga.

'Behave yourself darling' rapped her sister' it's not funny. You are only poking fun at the Guides because you were thrown out of the Brownies for doing a pas de deux when you were supposed to be dancing round the mushroom.'

'Then what was an elderly woman doing at a Guide camp site?' asked Olga.

'It seems there were a group of older women who belong to something called FG2 and they were holding a singalong and barbecue. It was one of them who was killed.'

'Perhaps she sang out of tune' grinned Olivia.

'It was probably someone who thought he could rob one of these old women and it turned nasty' said Norman Alkham who came across to the table where the others were sitting.

'The radio didn't say how she died' replied Trevor.

'Probably the proverbial blunt instrument' Olga said 'it's the sort of thig these thugs do. They set out to rob someone and hit them so hard the poor thing dies.'

At this point the door opened and the Reverend Donald Craigton held the door open for Megan Legge.

'Good morning everyone' he said with smile. 'I came across Megan just coming out of the doctor's surgery and I thought she could probably use something to brighten her day.'

'Are you feeling poorly Megan?' asked Olga.

'Not particularly 'Megan replied 'I had a rather nasty migraine the day before yesterday and I thought I would have a check-up with the doctor. Also, my ankle has been playing me up.'

'You poor thing' Olivia patted her arm 'are you feeling better today?'

'Yes thanks. These things don't last long. I just shut myself up in peace and quiet until it goes away.'

'I went past your place that evening' said Trevor and the house appeared to be in darkness.

'It would be. I was in bed without any light on and Walter was at a Law Society dinner.'

'What's the problem with your ankle Megan? Said Olivia

'Oh, it's an old injury that I did years ago that comes back to haunt me from time to time. The doctor gives me some pain killers and ointment and that eases it.'

'Did you hear about this other murder Donald?' asked Olga.

'The one out near Horsham? Yes, I did. A woman in her sixties apparently. I saw Constable Watson earlier and he told me about it. It seems the victim was attending a Guide function at a campsite. She was a retired Guider.'

'You were a Guider Megan, weren't you?' asked Olivia. 'Did you know her?'

'I hadn't heard about this until now' replied Megan.

'Her name was apparently Audrey Hope' said Donald. 'Did you know her Megan?'

'Audrey Hope? Yes, I did know her. We're both members of FG2.'

'Were you due to be that the same meeting?' asked Trevor.

'Yes, I was but I had to cry off because of my migraine.'

'Lucky for you' whistled Olga,' or it could have been you that was batted over the head.'

'Is that how she died? asked Trevor.

'Constable Watson said something about a stabbing' said Donald.

'Just like our own murder 'cried Olivia, 'I do hope there isn't a serial killer about.'

'Don't be so melodramatic darling' said her sister 'just finish up your drink before you get a fit of the heebie jeebies.'

Donald Craigton was seated at his desk working on the next Sunday's sermon when Harold Whitehouse knocked on the door and entered.

'Excuse me my lord but there is a lady asking to see you.'

'What name did she give Harold?'

'Miss Alison Oakes. She was a friend of the late Mr Burgess my lord.'

'Ah yes, I have heard of her but not met her. Show her in please Harold.'

He was immediately impressed by the woman who entered. She was quite attractive and was dressed in a formal grey suit and white blouse.

'Good afternoon Miss Oakes' he held out his hand and received a firm response. 'Please sit down. Now how can I be of assistance?'

'To be quite frank Reverend Craigton I find myself in a difficult position. I was, as you may know, a close friend of Nigel Burgess. Not to put too fine a point on it we lived together at The Great Barn for several months. However, our relationship had come to an end, by mutual agreement I would hasten to add, and I was about to leave the village for my home in Itchenor when Nigel was killed.'

'That must have been a terrible experience for you.'

'It wasn't very nice that's for sure. The thing is that his partners in the firm in Chichester think that, as he did not have any family, I should be the one who should organise the funeral. They feel that it is right and proper that he should have a suitable funeral and that as the person closest to Nigel before his death I am the one who should organise it.'

'Have funeral directors been instructed Miss Oakes?'

'Yes, its Finlaysons in Chichester.'

'Will they not make the necessary arrangements?'

'They will but they need to know what is required of them.'

' Of course '

'You see Reverend Craigton I have never had to do anything like this before and am somewhat like a fish out of water. I was hoping you might be able to offer some help.'

'I am happy to do anything I can to be assistance. Let me ask you some questions. Firstly, is it intended that there be a church funeral or a ceremony at the crematorium?'

'I think they want a church funeral with all the bells and whistles.'

'Do they want that to be here in the village?'

'I think so, after all this is where he lived.'

'When you say the full bells and whistles does that mean you would want the choir and the organ and the bell to be tolled?'
'If that is what is usually done.'
'If you wish I can arrange for all that to be done. The next question is who do you wish to officiate and what order of service would you like?'
'Could you officiate?'
'I could if you wish but it may be that in view of his importance you may wish it to be the Rector if he is available.'
'As they left me to make the arrangements, I would prefer it if it was you. I have no idea about an order of service or how to go about it.'

Donald open a drawer in his desk and drew out a leaflet.

'This is the service order for a funeral conducted here a couple of years ago. It sets out the general format. The choice of music and readings will have to be personal for Mr Burgess and it will also be necessary to decide if anyone is to give a funeral oration. If there is no-one to do this then I shall need some background information about Mr. Burgess when I give the address. Once you have done this you can give this pro forma and your choices of music etc to the funeral directors and they will arrange the printing and sending out of invitations.'
'Thank you that's is a great help. I can discuss the music etc with my mother who is a member of a church choir.'
'Now, will you want there to be sides men or women provided by the church?'
'If you think that is necessary'
'Not necessarily essential but it can make things run more smoothly. I can arrange for that if you wish.'
'Thank you.'
'That leaves the question of burial or cremation. Our churchyard is full I am afraid. However, if you wish interment the best people to ask are the funeral directors. They can advise on that option or make arrangements with the crematorium. If the latter is chosen then, after the service, I and anyone who so wishes will accompany the hearse to the crematorium and I will pronounce the committal.'
'Thank you so much. You have taken quite a load from my shoulders.'
'If you have any additional questions or problems then do not hesitate to contact me. Oh, and one final point. If there are to be after funeral refreshments you will need to decide if this will be done at the house or at The Six Bells.'
'I will certainly take you up on that offer if the need arises' she then paused and added,' I wonder if I might raise another point.'
'Of course, you may.'
'Its just that I get the impression that the police, or at least Inspector Love, suspect me of killing Nigel. Needless to say, I did no such thing.'

'If they do seem to think that it is likely to be because you found him. It is not unknown for the person who does that turns out to be the killer. Also, of course, you were in the process of ending a relationship with him. The best advice I can offer is to answer any questions honestly and not to answer questions that are not asked. I imagine that once the police are satisfied with your alibi you will cease to be a person of interest.'
'Thank you for that advice.'
'I don't suppose that you have any idea as to who might be responsible?' Donald asked casually.'
'None at all. Nigel was a self-made man and he was the type who, while he may not have done anything illegal, could well have cut corners or may have frustrated or cut out a rival. He had a ruthless streak in his make up.'

Sergeant Grant pulled up outside a semi-detached housing association property in Crawley. He accompanied by a young female detective constable Laura Portman.

'I will ask the main questions Laura' he said, 'you make the notes, keep a close watch on him and his reactions and pop in the odd question if you think it helps.'

The door to the house was opened by a young man with a very short hair cut, who needed a shave. He was wearing jeans and a tee shirt with a racing car pictured on the front.

'Norman Vale?' Grant asked.

'Yes, what do you want?'

Grant introduced himself and constable Portman and asked if they could step inside for a few minutes. Somewhat reluctantly Vale agreed. A young woman with fair hair and wearing slacks and a tee shirt came out of what Grant assumed was the kitchen.

'Sergeant Grant and Constable Portman ' Grant said ' we need to ask Mr Vale a few questions.'

'What about? 'Vale demanded 'I haven't done anything.'

'Its information we are after Vale. You work for Mobile Caterers, don't you?'

'Yep, that's right. It's a part time job. My main work is in a factory out near the airport.'

'You were part of a team of people who went to Girl Guide camp site a couple of evenings ago?'

'That's right. A lot of old biddies singing songs round a bonfire and we provided hot dogs and burgers. What about it?'

'Haven't you heard that one of the ladies who was there was stabbed to death?'

'Get away! 'Vale exclaimed 'who did that?'

'That is what we are trying to find out. Does the name Audrey Hope mean anything to you?'

'Can't say it does.'

'That's odd because you were sent to prison for eighteen months for assaulting her.'

'I did my time and have gone straight ever since. I've a good job and I work part time because we are saving for a deposit on a house. We have a baby daughter.'

'Audrey Hope was the person killed.'

'Now look you can't lay that on to me. I never seen her there. I was too busy working and besides all those old biddies looked the same to me.'

'But when you were convicted you said you would get her when you got out.'

'What of it? I was upset. That bitch of a Gloria Turner had pinched all my savings and blown them on clothes and handbags. I was hopping mad and was teaching the thieving bitch a lesson when this old biddy set about me with her umbrella. I just hit out to protect myself. Anyhow that's all a long time ago. I got a right rollicking from my probation officer for saying that. I never gave the thing another thought. When I got out, I found work and met Emma here. Now you come along and try to accuse me of topping that old biddy. I suppose its easy to pick on someone with a record.'
'Take it easy Vale no-one is accusing you of anything. Just tell me what you did that evening.'
'I was picked up from here about six thirty and drove out in the van to this camp site. We set up our gear ready to serve the food at eight o'clock. I was on cooking veggie burgers and sausages. When there was an order, I put it up, bread roll and onions and tomato sauce or mustard if they wanted it. After they had their food we cleaned up, packed up and came home. I was here just after ten.'
'Were you with anyone all evening ?'
'Course I was. We was all crowded in the van. Five of us. Two of us were cooking and the others serving. When we was done the cooks cleaned up and the others gathered up the waste. I will say this the old biddies were tidy and they didn't have to go looking for rubbish. Ask any of the others and they will tell you I was with them the whole time.'
'I will do that. In the meantime I want you to call in at the local police station and they will take a formal statement and get you to sign it . Any questions constable?'
'I don't think so sir.'

Outside Grant asked
'What do you make of that?'
'I'd say he was telling the truth. I was watching his face all the time. He gave no sign of being nervous or of lying.'
'I agree. Provided his story is borne out by the others I think we can rule our Norman Vale.'

The other members of the Mobile catering staff who were on duty at the camp site told exactly the same story as Norman Vale and it was clear that he had at no time been on his own during the whole of their trip to the site, their work there and their trip home. Whoever killed Audrey Hope it was not Norman Vale.

During the following days a team of workers received and collated the statements made by the members of FG who had attended the camp fire and barbecue. A number of them remembered seeing Audrey Hope during the evening, of sitting next to her or close to her and, in some cases of talking with her. There was a need to go back to some of the people to double check what they had said and to eliminate any errors in memory. One thing that was clear was that no-one recalled seeing Audrey Hope after the refreshment break. The owners of cars parked near hers had noted that she was still on the site but none of them thought this was anything out of the ordinary. Equally important was the fact that none of those who had been there could recall seeing anyone who was other than a member of FG2. They had all been wearing the same sweatshirt so anyone not dressed in one would have stood out like a sore thumb. The only exception that some mentioned was Mrs Agar the Warden who was wearing a blue Guide sweatshirt. Whilst there were gaps in the information given, not everyone was with someone else the whole time it was impossible to identify anyone whose story was completely out of line. It seemed unlikely on the evidence available that it was another of those present who had killed Audrey Hope.

CHAPTER 16

Donald Craigton satisfied himself that the visit he was about to make was recorded in his diary he opened the kitchen door and told Harold Whitehouse that he was leaving.

'Very good my lord" came the reply from the larder. 'Have you any idea when you might return if anyone should ask ?'
'I may be out for a couple of hours.'

The weather was fine so Donald merely picked up the book he had bought and set off. He made his way across the village green and down the street towards the main road. After about a quarter of a mile he tuned off to the left into a side road of modern detached and semi-detached houses. The one he wanted was at the far end and was the home of Tony and Brenda Clifton who had added an extension to the house to provide accommodation for Brenda's father Arnold Treacher and it was Arnold that Donald had come to visit. His knock at the front door was answered by a woman in her late forties with grey hair and brown eyes.
'Good afternoon Brenda' he said 'I have called to see your father. Is it convenient?'
'Good afternoon Mr Craigton' she smiled stepping aside ' come along in Dad will be pleased to see you.'

She led him down the hallway and opened a door on the right.
'Here's Mr Craigton to see you dad' she said and closed the door behind Donald.
The room he entered was bright and modern and looked out over the garden with a view of the downs as a backdrop.
'How are you today Arnold?'
'Not too bad Mr Craigton thank you, but I have to say I would be happier if I didn't have this blessed arthritis.'

Arnold Treacher had been a tall and upright man whose appearance underlined the fact that he had spent all his life outdoors. His face was still ruddy and his white hair showed that it had been hidden most of his life under a cap. The gnarled knuckles on his hand showed the effects of the arthritis that kept him forced to pass nearly all his time in his special armchair. Though his face showed the physical discomfort he suffered his eyed were bright and he had a ready smile.

'Its good to see you. I don't get many visitors these days.'
'I have brought something you might find interesting Arnold' Donald said holding out the book he had brought.
 "Southdown Sheep and Their Shepherds" 'said Arnold his eyes lighting up. 'I shall enjoy reading this. How did you come by it? Its not a new publication is it?'
'No, it was printed fifty years ago and I found it on a stall in Chichester market. When I read the title, I thought that I knew just the man who would enjoy it.'
'I'll let you have it back when I've finished it.'
'No need to do that. You keep it. You'll get more pleasure from it than anyone else I know. After all you were a shepherd all your working life'
'Its amazing how much the world has changed in the last fifty year' Arnold said flicking through some of the photos in the book. 'Not only sheep farming but everything.'
'I expect the village was quite a bit different when you were a young man.'
'It was that. Looking at it now you would never think that there was a general store that sold everything from nails to ladies' nighties. Added to which there was a butcher cum fishmonger and a blacksmith. The pub only sold beer, none of this fancy food and wines. Not only that but people didn't have cars, they had to rely on using a bicycle or catch the weekly charabanc into Chichester. There was no wireless then and certainly no television. For entertainment there were black and white silent films in the village hall once a week or you had to make your own entertainment. The village had a football team and a cricket team. In addition, there used to be regular whist drives and jumble sales and every year we had a big Fete on the green. Given the long hours we had to work we didn't have time to get bored.'

At this point Brenda appeared with tea and biscuits. When settled with their cups and plates Donald said;
'You mentioned that there used to be a big Fete each year on the green. That's interesting because there is a move to organise something along those lines for this year or next. Can you remember exactly what form the Fete took?'
'It was a big event that went on for more than one day. There would be sports for the children and the adults, then there was always a visit from a travelling fair with its rides and sideshows. There was a flower show in the church and entertainments in the village hall. The last day was always a special event with people dressing up and all kinds of entertainments and competitions depending on the chosen topic.'
'It certainly sounds a big event.'
'You have to remember that people didn't have as many holidays then and could not afford to go away to places like France and Spain. It was all part of making your own amusements.'
'What kind of topics were there for these special event Arnold ?'

'All sorts. I remember one year it was pirates and smugglers and another it was Robin Hood. But it all came to an end with the war. I always remember the folk having to walk the plank when it was pirates to see if they fell into a tank of cold water. When it was Robin Hood they had an archery competition which was won by a young girl called Megan who outshot all the men. Those days were good fun and enjoyed by everyone.'
'Did the war have much effect here? Apart I mean for people having to go and join the forces.'
'The worst time was in 1940 when we were expecting the Germans to invade us.'
'Yes, we are not far from the coast here are we'
'Not many people know this and I am not sure we are allowed to talk about it but it was a long time ago now. 'Arnold said in a quiet voice 'It seems to me that it would be wrong if the facts died with those of us who knew about it. I reckon that telling you, a vicar, is as good as keeping it secret without the knowledge dying out. The thing is that plans were made for what was to happen if the Nazis did come. Special units were set up who were to stay behind and sabotage the German lines. These groups had secret hiding places so they could come out at night to cause problems by blowing up bridges and railways and things like that.'
'Was this the Home Guard ?'
'No these were secret groups whose names were known only to others in the group. They were people who knew the countryside like the back of their hands and who could get about quietly and secretly. When the Germans never came the whole thing was shut down as secretly as it was set up. Hardly anyone is left who knew about the local group.'
'There was one in the village?' Donald asked?
'Oh yes there was one here right enough. We had a secret hiding place not so far away. Also, and this will surprise you, the radio that was to be used to get orders and to communicate with other groups was kept in the church.'
'I never knew that. Where did they keep it?' Donald was surprised at this news as he tried to work out where you could hide a radio in that building.
'Under the altar with its aerial connected to the wires for the lightning conductor. The vicar was to be the radio operator.'
'And its been kept secret all this time ?'
'Yes, but I was thinking the other day that someone ought to know before the last of us departs this life. Mind you would have been surprised the sort of people who were involved.'
'Like you ?'
'That's right. They chose me because I knew the downs like the back of my hands. Then there were game keepers and poachers as well as some farmers. To get messages moved from one place to another they were hidden in strange places like behind notices on telephone poles. Someone would collect them and

deliver them to a secret place ready to be transmitted. This meant someone had to go out and about at night to pick up the messages. Here it was a young lass, the same one who was the champion archer, who rode her horse or her bike and collected the messages. You wouldn't think it was her today to see her now all middle aged and too fat even to ride a bike.'
'But there was never an invasion was there?'
'No, thank the Lord there was not. They told us our life expectancy would have been no more than two weeks if they had come. But when they didn't the whole thing was wound up.'
'Did you all join the Home Guard instead 'Donald asked.
'Some did while others were posted to the army where they joined special units.'
'What about you Arnold?'
'I joined the commandos, and ended up on the beach on D-Day. It was bit different from being a shepherd I can tell you Mr Craigton.'
'I bet it was. 'And in an effort to lighten the mood Craigton added 'And what about the young girl and her horse, did they return to hunting foxes?'
'Not that I know of. As a matter of fact, she more or less disappeared from the village for the duration. She's never told what she was doing. Even young girls ended up doing the most surprising jobs during those years. Jobs they have never talked about to this day.'

Donald found himself looking at the village and its inhabitants with new eyes as he returned home

'Chief Superintendent Buxton. A pleasure to see you sir' greeted Harold Whitehouse 'are you wishing to see his lordship?'
'If possible, Harold, is he at home?'
'Not at the moments sir. He is delivering some Parish Magazines. One of the usual people is unwell and his lordship has agreed to deputise. I expect him back in about ten minutes. Would you care to come in and wait?'
'Thank you 'Buxton stepped past Harold into the hallway.' 'While I am waiting, I am wondering if you have heard anything on the village grapevine that might shed any light on this killing?'
'Nothing of any significance sir. The funeral attracted a good deal of short-term interest. I don't think anything like it had been seen in Upper Burford in the last one hundred years. Most of the local people had no idea who the great majority of the mourners were. There were only a few of the local residents who attended although quite a number gathered outside to observe the function.'
'What about the crime and who was responsible?'
'A lot of generally wild speculation ranging from the young lady who lived at the house to any one of the people who had visited the deceased at his house or even one of his business associates. But no-one, as far as I am aware, has any definitive information '

At this point voices could be heard approaching the house and Donald Craigton entered together with two ladies who, if Buxton had not heard about the Misses Olivia and Olga Sanderson, might have caused him to think he was seeing double.

'Richard' cried Donald extending his hand ' an unexpected pleasure. May I introduce Olivia and Olga Sanderson. This, ladies is Chief Superintendant Richard Buxton of the Sussex Police, Richard and I met a long time ago when I was a government employee.'
'Pleased to meet you' said Richard offering a hand to each of the ladies who were dressed in emerald green dresses with a matching short jacket and green, high heeled shoes.
'Have you come to put us through the third degree like Inspector Love? asked Olivia.
'I am afraid I left my thumbscrew back at the office 'smiled Richard at which both ladies had a fit of the giggles.
'Seriously though' said Olga 'do you know who did kill that dreadful man?'
'You think he was dreadful, do you?'

'How else would you describe a man who was rude to everyone he met and made no bones about that fact that he thought we were all living a hundred years ago touching our forelocks to the squire and the vicar.'
'You had better be careful what you are saying darling 'said Olivia nudging her sister in the ribs 'or the Chief Superintendent will be adding you to his list of suspects.'
'Who is to say you are not already on it 'grinned Donald Craigton.
'There you are, what did I tell you darling 'said Olivia.
'Actually, Miss Olga I have seen you before. 'said Buxton 'My late wife was a keen ballet fan and one year I took her to see you dancing in Coppelia. Quite a night out for a Detective Constable in those days.'
'I hope she enjoyed the performance 'said Olga.
'Very much. In fact, we both did.'
'Just so this isn't too one sided 'Donald added 'I can recall hearing a record in a coffee bar of Olivia singing with the Ted Heath Band.'
'Heavens above that was an absolute age ago 'cried Olivia.
'Come on darling before more of our murky past is revealed. If you will let us have those leaflets Donald, we will see they get put through the necessary doors.'
'Bless you Olga that will be a great help. 'he went over to a side table and took up a small bundle of leaflets which he gave to Olga.
'Come on darling. Let's go and play postmen and leave these two to reminisce about days gone by.'

When they had left the room and been shown out by Harold the curate turned to his guest and said 'What do you make of those two? They certainly liven up the village but, at the same time, they have very generous natures. Olivia coaches the choir when there is an anthem and Olga gives ballet lessons to little girls.'
'One look at those two side by side is enough to make any man sign the pledge' laughed Buxton.
'What brings you here today Richard?'
'I was in the area and thought I would pop in for a chat.'
'How is the investigation going? '
'Slowly, but its far more complex than one might imagine. Our Mr Burgess seems to have had a lot of different irons in the fire all of which have to be checked out.'
'If my reading of the man was right, I suspect that you may have found out that he wasn't exactly a knight in shining armour.'
'People who make a lot of money in a short time never are as you well know Donald.'
'Does this mean that the perpetrator is more likely to be someone outside the village?'

'We haven't got that far. One of the problems is that he lived what you may call two lives. One of them was in the village where he showed a considerable ability to upset and offend practically everyone he came into contact with. The other was a pretty wide variety of business interests which almost certainly gained him enemies and people who had old scores to settle.'

'I have no knowledge nor do I wish to have any about his external activities and, as I have already told you, I am not willing to act as a police informer on village affairs. You have a local constable who probably knows as much, if not more, than I do about the people who live here.'

'All the same Donald you were a highly experienced police officer and I suspect that it's not in your nature to not apply that knowledge and experience to this case. After all, to have an unsolved murder in a small village like this must create uncertainty and worries among the population. How do people know that whoever it was who killed Burgess will not strike again? '

'They don't and I admit that his death has created some tensions in the village. You can't stop people speculating and what starts out as "I wonder if A or B" rapidly becomes ' Have you heard that A or B did so and so. That is why it is important that you do catch the killer.'

'Easier said than done Donald. We are gradually whittling down the list but there are still plenty of possibilities. The situation is not made any easier by the fact that we have a second killing using the same MO and a connection between the two is proving hard to find.'

'Are you certain it's the same person in both cases?'

'The forensic evidence points clearly in that direction. The odds of two separate people using the same weapon, and all the evidence is that it was the same weapon, must be remote to say the least. And that is a piece of information that is not for general circulation.'

'Which means that you are looking for links between the two victims'

'Exactly and that is by no means easy. 'said Buxton ' Audrey Hope was in her sixties. She was a retired school teacher and Girl Guide leader. It seems she was more than a bit old fashioned in her views on society. One of her external interests was politics where she seems to have been a right-wing Tory. The only other thing that makes her somewhat out of the ordinary is that she was a great lover of Switzerland, its people and its way of life. She went there every year. In fact, she worked there for a couple of years before the war. Oh, and she knew Nigel Burgess but seems to have got on quite well with him. There is nothing there that suggests an obvious motive for murder.'

'You say that she seems to have got on well with Burgess. Does that imply that their deaths were related?'

'Do you mean that she knew something that pointed to the Burgess killer and so had to be removed herself?'

'It's a possibility even if it is remote.'

'From what I know of her I can't think she ever had anything to do with the dodgier activities of Burgess or would even know anyone who was involved with them.'

'So, I suppose you will be quizzing all people you questioned before to see if they have an alibi?'

'Of course.'

'I might be able to save you some time 'grinned Craigton. 'You see the evening that the murder took place was the evening on which the local committee that runs the village hall had a meeting. I was there and so was Trevor Nightingale and the two ladies you met a short while ago. So, we can alibi each other. Oh, and you will be pleased to know that Verity Trumper was in the chair so there is no need to bother her which will no doubt be good news for your CC. The only one not there was Megan Legge and she was confined to her bed with a bad migraine and isolated in a darkened room all that day and night. This was confirmed by Walter Legge who was going to a Law Society Dinner. If need be, I will give you a statement to that effect.

'Thank you, Donald that would be a help. You have saved your friends, and yourself, from another grilling from Inspector Love'

'When I tell them that' laughed Donald 'it's going to cost them a drink.'

'Which makes it look as if the crimes were not related even if they were carried out by the same person.'

'I am not absolutely sure I would go that far. You know Richard villages like this are not the same as towns or cities.'

'I think we have sussed that one out for ourselves.'

'What I mean is that the pace of life is slower here than in Chichester or Brighton. Not only the pace of life but the pace of change. This can mean that to understand what happens in a small village you may have to accept that its roots go back much further than would be the case in a large town. Memories can be longer and slower to come to the boil in places like this.'

'But Burgess was a comparative newcomer here. As far as we know he had never set foot in the place before he bought The Great Barn. He had no history here.'

'What about the woman? Did she have any connection with this place?'

'No direct connection as far as we know.'

'You mentioned the Girl Guides. We have only Brownie Guides here nowadays but there have been Girl Guides in the past.'

'I can't see Burgess being killed because he wanted to re-site a Guide Hall or that Audrey Hope was killed because she agreed with this proposal.'

'Both these facts may be as you say but it does not make my comment inappropriate. All I am saying, and I have no proof to support this, is that it is just possible the event that underlies both these killings has its birth not today nor in the recent past. Its just a thought but I felt it may be useful to pass on to you.'

'It's an interesting thought I grant you that.'
 'I did say it was a remote chance. So, what do you do now? Be like Mr Micawber and hope something turns up? '
'I don't t think I have reached that stage yet' laughed Buxton.

CHAPTER 18

At the Chief Superintendent's suggestion Inspector Thomasson tracked down Colonel Frederick Ball the secretary of the Mid Weald Conservative Association at their headquarters in what had formally been a gentleman's hairdressers but was now the Committee Rooms of the Association. A telephone call had ascertained that the colonel would be available that afternoon so Thomasson drove over to Lingfield. On arrival at the Committee Rooms he was shown into a small office that contained a desk, a filing cabinet and two plain wooden seats. On the wall behind the desk, at which the colonel was seated, was a large photograph of Margaret Thatcher.

'I am sorry to trouble you colonel but we are still trying to clarify the reason why Miss Audrey Hope was killed. Unless we can do that, it will make the task of finding who did so that much more difficult.'

'It seems to me' the colonel almost barked 'that the answer to that question is quite obvious.'

'How do you mean sir?'

'I mean that it must have been some passing thug who was bent on stealing whatever he could find or robbing anyone who was vulnerable. What you are looking for Inspector is an out and out thug. The death penalty should never have been revoked. The thought of the rope was enough to make most of these people stop and think before they beat old ladies over the head.'

'The problem is colonel that here has been nothing reported as being stolen that evening and no-one else was attacked or molested which tends to increase the chances that the murder was premeditated.'

'Damn it all man, who would want to kill Audrey Hope ?'

'That is what we are trying to find out sir. You took away all the papers you could find about Miss Hope's role as Treasurer of your Association. Can I take it that you are satisfied that the records and everything else associated with Miss Hope's role are in full order?'

'You most certainly can' the colonel thumped his desk. 'Miss Hope was the epitome of reliability and honesty. Her records were maintained in an immaculate manner and every last penny is fully accounted for. She will be sadly missed by this Association.'

'Did Miss Hope, to your knowledge eve run for elected office colonel ?'

'Wasn't her scene. We could have found her a safe seat on the local or even the county council but she was not interested in elected office. She felt that she could best serve the party in other ways.'

'Although she was not an elected representative, I presume that she played an active part in the affairs of the Association; canvassing for candidates, being on duty at polling stations and at the vote counting, that kind of thing.'

'You presume correctly Inspector. Audrey was a tireless worker for the party at a local level.'

'Did this ever bring her into conflict with people of other political persuasions?'
'Anyone who canvasses for votes or attends party meetings must expect, from time to time, to be confronted by people who have strong counter views. Its par for the course.'
'Does the name of the Army of the Proletarian Republic ring any bells colonel?'
'It sounds vaguely familiar. Why do you ask?'
'I have been told that an organisation of that name did contest some local and general elections about ten years ago and that their policies were extremely radical.'
'Yes, now you mention it there was a rag bag group of that name who sprouted up in the area at about the time. Like all these way-out groups they spend more time fighting among themselves than they do trying to win over voters. They have hardly arrived before they fall apart and are never heard of again. What's your interest in that rabble?'
'I am told that one of the leading lights of this APR was a man called Cooper who happened to be a teacher at the same school as Miss Hope.'
'Are you suggesting that this man could be responsible for her death?'
'I am not suggesting anything sir I am merely trying to get at the facts. Do you remember the man called Cooper?'
'Very vaguely. You need to understand that over the years you get all sorts of people standing in elections, all of whom have absolutely no chance of getting elected. The main parties tend to ignore these fringe people and concentrate on each other. As I remember this APR were about as far to the left as its possible to be. The nearest comparison I can think of is anarchists because they wanted to do away with all forms of government and law and order as well as the monarchy. Its hardly surprising they got so few votes.'
'I was told that at the general election Miss Hope was there as a representative of your party.'
'Most probably. We have our people at the count so that we can keep an eye on things and satisfy ourselves that everything is done according to the rules.'
'I gather also that Cooper was there and that he was not entirely sober.'
'No. The man was drunk and I told the Returning Officer he should have been thrown out of the count. His so-called speech when the result was announced was not far short of treasonable.' The colonel almost shouted.
'Do you know if he said anything in particular to you or to any of your party representatives?'
'Audrey Hope told me that he had said to her that when they gained power the gutters would run red with the blood of fascists like her. Very wisely she simply turned her back on him and walked away.'
'I see. Do you know if there was any further contact between Miss Hope and this man Cooper?'.

'As far as I can recall that was the last time we ever heard of him. Got better things to do than bother about scum like that.'
'You have been most helpful colonel. As I am sure that you understand it is necessary, in a case such as this, to get to understand the victim. By doing that you increase the chances of finding the perpetrator. I should be very grateful therefore for any information you feel able to give me regarding Miss Hope.'
'I wouldn't claim to have known her well but I believe I am a good judge of character. Had to be when you had charge of a large number of men. 'proclaimed the colonel brushing his moustache with his finger. 'What do you want to know ?'
'How would you sum her up as a person sir ?'
'She believed in what today are called outdated standards. You knew your place in society and respected your betters. You were properly self disciplined and you worked hard. None of this nonsense about the world owing you anything.'
'How do you think that fitted in with her non political activities sir?'
'It fitted very well. She may have demanded high standards but, you know, people rise to the challenge that sets. She was an excellent teacher at the school where she worked and a very popular leader for the Girl Guide movement. She might have been seen by some as old fashioned but she considered the British Empire, when we still had one, a force for good in the world. It brought with it responsibilities not only in the Empire but in Europe as well. We held the balance of power there for century and should have continued to do so. She had little time for the policies of the United States and no time at all for those of France. In her view this country made a bad mistake in 1919 in not ensuring a more equitable peace. She blamed Lloyd George for that. The way the Germans reacted to the Versailles Treaty was hardly surprising. Even so, if we had kept up our military strength and given proper support to the German monarchists the excesses of the Nazis could have been avoided. She supported several bodies that worked to try and bring about a better relationship with Germany. Above all she opposed communism or bolshevism as she called it. By failing to support the monarchists in Germany we had brought the second war on our own heads. Hitler, who was only in power because of Versailles, had to be stopped but she was sure the biggest threat to our way of life came from the Soviets. She was a firm supporter of our present prime minister and of the current president of the United States in their readiness to confront the evils of bolshevism. She was totally opposed to the rise in the power of the unions and to everything that she saw as weakening the moral fibre of this country. She watched with dismay the decline in the moral standards and the loss of power that had come to colour British life.'
'I believe that she had a particular affection for Switzerland.'

'Quite so 'agreed the colonel' she spent some time in that country in the late
thirties and retained her affection for Switzerland and its people and way of life.
She visited the country as often as she could.'
'Do you happen to know what she did during the war colonel ?'
'She told me that she had a clerical role in the Foreign Office where her fluency
in the German language was of assistance to her country.
'Thank you very much for your help colonel. I appreciate your finding time to
talk to me.'
'Always pleased to try and help the forces of law and order Inspector' the
colonel got to his feet and straightened his blue blazer. For a moment
Thomasson thought he was going to click his heels and give him a salute.

The inquest into the death of Nigel Burgess had been brief. Buxton had spoken to the coroner who had agreed to take only evidence of identity and the medical evidence. He would then ask if the police wanted an adjournment which he would grant. Everything went according to plan. The village hall at Upper Burford had been packed with locals anxious to pick up any snippets of information available and hoping against hope for some dramatic development. Alison Oakes, dressed in a smart navy-blue suit with white blouse, confirmed that the deceased was Nigel Burgess. Dr Penrose gave evidence that death had been due to a single blow from a narrow-bladed knife. Death had been instantaneous. Whereupon the coroner asked if the police were seeking an adjournment and when this was confirmed by Inspector Love he brought the hearing to close much to the disappointment of the audience who were deprived of any excitement. The one positive result was that the coroner issued a burial certificate and the funeral could now take place.

The inquest into the death of Audrey Hope was held in the Magistrate Court in Emsworth. Again, there was a good attendance from local inhabitants who were looking for an afternoon's entertainment. Most of them had little or no idea as to who Audrey Hope had been but murders were a rarity in the town and this new experience was not to be missed. Evidence of identification was given by Mrs Janet Davidson the Girl Guide County Commissioner which, in itself, caused a minor stir in the court room. She was wearing her official Guide uniform which seemed to add status to herself and importance to her evidence. The medical evidence was given once again by Doctor Penrose who confirmed that death was due to a single blow from a narrow-bladed knife. Before the jury had a chance to ask any questions the coroner adjourned the inquest to allow police enquiries to continue. The burial certificate was issued so that the funeral could be held.

Nigel Burgess' funeral was the first to take place. Alison Oakes, with the assistance of the funeral directors and the Reverend Donald Craigton had risen to the challenge. It was to be the biggest and most luxurious funeral that any inhabitant of the village could recall. Buxton had decided not attend the funeral but to keep it under observation to see who attended and what, if anything transpired. He had arranged for a police photographer to be among the press and television photographers so that he could photograph everyone who was at the funeral. Buxton, together with Inspector Love, were seated in a car so that they had a good view of the attendees. He had chosen Love because of his knowledge of local worthies. He had instructed him to point out particularly anyone whose name had come out as a result of Sergeant Barnett's enquiries. Constable Watson was more than fully occupied in sorting out parking for the many large and expensive cars that brought the mourners to the village. The church bells began to toll five minutes before the funeral was due to start. Almost to the second a very large hearse preceded by an undertaker in a black coat and top hat and carrying a long black handled and silver knobbed stick walked majestically down the middle of the road. At the church gate the undertaker stopped, removed his hat, walked to the side of the hearse and bowed his head. This was a signal for the bearers in the following car to descend and to open the rear door of the hearse to remove the coffin on to their shoulders. The passengers in the dozen or so following cars formed up behind the coffin which was now on the shoulders of the bearers. A robed clergyman arrived and led the procession into the church where the other attendees were already in place. Buxton could just make out Donald Craigton's voice as he led the procession down the aisle and the church doors were closed.

'Very impressive 'Buxton said. 'Did you recognise many of those who were in the procession?'
'Quite a lot of them sir 'replied Love. There was Walter Legg the lawyer
plus the man who has taken over as chairman of the estate agency together with several other directors. There were one or two others who were mentioned by Sergeant Barnett as well.'
'You will be able to confirm all that when we get the photographs. Now what I am interested in is anyone who is not a part of the official funeral but is here to see what is going on. Not just the local rubber necks but strangers. Slip out and have a word with Constable Watson and ask him to keep any eye on the people forming up in the churchyard and round the gate and see if there is anyone he does not recognise. If he does, he is to let you know.'
'Wont that draw attention to our car sir ?'
'No, because I want you to also keep an eye on the crowd. If Watson has anything to report he can reach you more easily that way. Pay particular attention to those in the church as well as those standing around outside.'

Buxton did not tell Love that he had arranged for Sergeant Sparrow to be in the church to see whether there was anyone that he knew or thought was behaving suspiciously. It wasn't beyond the realms of possibility that if there was a random killer, he might be tempted to see the end result of his work. While the service was in process the bearers appeared from a side door and removed the wreaths from the hearse and its roof and from a second hearse which was filled with flowers. These were laid out on the grass of the churchyard. After some forty minutes the church doors opened and a man carrying a gold cross exited followed by the Reverend Craigton and then the bearers with the coffin on their shoulders. The leading mourner followed and stood by as the coffin was replaced in the hearse. Then the bearers returned to their car and were joined by the priest and it and four other vehicles containing the leading mourners drove off. Those not going to the crematorium were exiting the church and invited mourners were making their way across to The Red Bull where refreshments were being served. The uninvited attendees and the members of the public crowded around the floral tributes not that many if any of them would be any the wiser if they could read the cards identifying the sender. Slowly the village started to empty.

'Well?' said Buxton to Love when the latter came back to the car. 'Anything interesting?'
'There was one man who didn't seem to fit in. According to Watson he is not a villager. He's a dark, swarthy looking chap. Italian or Greek most likely. I told Watson to keep an eye on him.'
'Look there is Sparrow' Buxton pointed 'I had him inside the church. Get him to trail this man and if he leaves in a car to get the make and registration number. We don't want to lose him.'

When Sparrow came back to the car her reported that he had shadowed the man to his car, an expensive Audi, and taken its number which had been passed on to the authorities for details of the registered owner. He had another piece of information to provide.

'There was a woman in the church whose face seemed vaguely familiar but I couldn't place it. Maybe it was the hair style or the fact that she was older than the person I had in my mind. It was only as they were carrying the coffin out of the church that I saw her at a different angle and I remembered who she is or rather who she was. Her name, when I had last seen her, was Naomi Burgess. She was Nigel's wife. I was a new constable on my first beat about ten years ago. One of the older men pointed her out to me as the wife of the up and coming businessman who had walked out on him for someone more reliable, fed up, according to gossip, with his penchant for busty blondes. Because she left him, he divorced her on grounds of her adultery. I thought she had left the area years ago.'
'So, he had an ex-wife who was unlikely to be his biggest fan.' Said Buxton 'It could have galled her to see how wealthy he had become. I think we had better trace her and see where she was the night Burgess died.'
'What about the other fellow sir?'
'When we know who he is we can decide if he needs to be followed up. It seems that Burgess had an ever-increasing list of people who had cause to wish him ill.'

The second funeral was held in the parish church in Emsworth. It was a much smaller affair than the ostentatious display of mock grief for Nigel Burgess. The mourners who made their way into the church divided themselves between friends and acquaintances, members of the Girl Guide movement especially those who came wearing a FG2 tee shirt and local inhabitants who came because they attended every funeral or wanted to see who else was there. There was just the hearse but no following cars. The vicar welcomed it at the door and led the way into the building saying the opening words of the service. Among those who waited outside was Inspector Thomasson who noted the arrival of the County Commissioner, Mrs Davidson, Colonel Ball with another elderly man obviously representing the Conservative Party and Mr Westwood and Mr Martin from the school. While he was waiting Thomasson looked at the other bystanders and, noticing a man who did not appear to be a local, he wandered in his direction as if he too was no more than a watcher. After acknowledging Thomasson's presence by his side, the man turned to look directly at him and gave a slight nod of his head.

'Kurt Schneider' he said and held out a hand 'I am from Zurich in Switzerland '
'Robert Thomasson and I am from Horsham in Sussex' he replied.
'You have known her a long time?'
'No' replied Thomasson but did not enlarge on that reply.
'I have not gone into the church because I am a Roman Catholic ' Herr Schneider said.
'I understand.'
'I am here because I have known Audrey Hope nearly all my life.'
'Is that so 'Thomasson tried to sound non-committal.'
'Yes, my father employed Audrey to teach me English when I was four years of age. It was 1937 and she was living in Zurich having just finished at university. When the war started two years later, she had to return to this country.'
'You lost touch with her during the war I suppose?'
'We did not see her again until 1946. This was despite the fact that my father was posted to the Swiss Embassy as a commercial attaché from 1942 to 1945. Audrey was working in London also but she did not know my father was there.'
'She came back to Zurich after the war? Was it to work? '
'No, she trained to be a teacher but she came on holiday to Switzerland every year after that. She was very attached to the Swiss way of life.'

At this point the church door opened and the coffin reappeared to be placed back in the hearse.

'Where do they take her now?' asked Her Schneider.
'To the local cemetery I understand.'
'Then I will find my car and follow her to her last resting place.' He put his hand in his pocket and drew out a business card. 'My card. If you are in Zurich please let me know and we can meet for a drink.'
'Thank you' replied Thomasson who held out one of his personal address cards.

Her Schneider shook his hand and gave him a bow of the head and hurried off to find his car. Thomasson watched him go and decided that he would let Chief Superintendent Buxton know of this additional information about Audrey Hope.

CHAPTER 20

The building in East Pallant looked more like a Georgian house than an office .
However, there was a brightly polished brass plate by the door that read "Oakes
Associates ". Chief Superintendent Buxton pressed the doorbell and waited. He
had decided that for this interview he would be accompanied by Sergeant
Sparrow. Given Inspector Love's fixation with the young woman's guilt he
wanted both of the people interviewing her to have an open mind. The door
clicked open and a female voice said
'Please come in '
They stepped into a tiled porch with another door in front of them. Buxton put
out his hand and the door opened and led them into a hallway with black and
white tiles on the floor, crimson red walls and a number of varnished mahogany
doors. The one on the left nearest them opened and a young woman dressed in a
black and white check dress and smart high heeled shoes came into the hallway.
'Can I help you?' she asked in a well educated voice.
'We are police officers' replied Buxton and they produced their credentials ' we
should like to speak to Miss Oakes please.'
'Do you have an appointment?'
'No but we still wish to speak to Miss Oakes.'
'Please take a seat in here 'she crossed the hallway and opened another door
into what was obviously a waiting room. It was furnished with two large and
deep leather chairs and a matching sofa. The floor was carpeted in a plain beige
carpet and the walls were painted cream. On the walls were a number of prints
of Chichester through the ages. A large window covered by a venetian blind
looked out on to the street. In the centre of the room was a coffee table with a
glass top on which were displayed a number of magazines and a copy of that
day's Times. The subdued lighting came from a number of electric lamps.

'If this room is anything to go by sir 'said Sparrow 'Miss Oakes runs a pretty
successful business.'
'So it would seem. Unless its window dressing.'

At this point the door opened a young woman in her thirties dressed in dark
grey business suit with a plain white blouse and well polished black shoes
entered.

'Good morning 'she held out a hand and had a warm smile on her face. 'I
recognise you Sergeant' she said to Sparrow and then turned to Buxton and
added 'but I don't think we have met.'
'Chief Superintendent Buxton 'he said showing her his credentials

'Pleased to meet you Chief Superintendent. Would you like to come through to my office'?

She led the way down the hall and into a room on the left. It had chestnut panelled walls and a deep red carpet and curtains. The walls displayed a number of pleasant watercolours. In the centre of the room was a large desk with several telephones and a computer screen as well as a green shaded desk lamp.

'Please sit down ' she sat in the big chair behind the desk and pointed to the two brown leather armchairs facing it. 'What can I do for you Chief Superintendent? I thought I had given such information as I had to Inspector Love.'
'You wont mind if the sergeant makes some notes of our conversation?'
'Not at all. 'she smiled ' I shall be recording this meeting myself' and she pressed a button on a keyboard by one of the phones.
'I have come to see you Miss Oakes because I believe that you knew the late Mr Burgess very well.'
'As much as anyone did Chief Superintendent. Nigel was not in the habit of being particularly forthcoming.'
'In a situation as this the police find it is necessary to learn as much as they can about the person who has been the victim of a crime. It is not a cliché to say that if you know the victim well enough you will discover the criminal. Did you in fact know that he had been married?'
'Yes I did. He made a point of telling me and of adding that he had no intention of making the same mistake twice. Just to let me know I need not get ideas in that direction.'
'Do you know the former Mrs Burgess?'
'No. I don't even know her name. He didn't say and I didn't ask.'
'Was he more forthcoming about his business affairs Miss Oakes?'
'If you mean did he take me into his confidence about them then the answer is no. Ours was a more personal relationship most of the time.'
'Most of the time?'
'It so happened that at one stage we both had space at a business development convention in London. Quite by chance we were both approached by a potential client. Nigel for his property management expertise and myself for my public relations skills. This led eventually to our being successful in obtaining business from the brewery group that I visited the day that Nigel was killed. In fact, I was told, as I left Canterbury, that Nigel was to be awarded the contract he had been negotiating. I tried to phone him but got no reply so I am afraid he died unaware of his success.'
'How much of his business activities did you know about?'
'I knew he was chairman and chief executive of the estate agent business, that allied to this he had companies that specialised in property management,

property investment and property development but I had no detailed knowledge of those activities.'

'Did you know, for example, the kind of properties in which he invested?' asked Sergeant Sparrow.'

'Only in very general terms. I can recall him pointing out some industrial premises that he said he owned and some retail premises as well but I couldn't identify them for you now. I paid only a passing interest.'

'How would you sum up Mr Burgess' approach to business ethics Miss Oakes'

'That is a very difficult question Chief Superintendent. I don't recall ever discussing business ethics with him.'

'But from what you did know how would you answer that question?'

'Nigel Burgess was a wealthy and successful business man. Anyone who gets as far as he had done by his age must have had a ruthless streak in him which means that he had probably cut some corners in his time. I very much doubt that you get his type of success by being a goody goody.'

'Would it surprise you to know, for example that he appears to have bribed certain people to grant him permissions he required?'

'Frankly it wouldn't. If Nigel wanted something, he went all out to get it. To be honest I think he believed in the eleventh commandment – Thou shall not be found out.'

'Then would it surprise you be told he appears to have been involved in other illegal activities?'

'Yes and no. On the one hand he never gave the impression that he approved of specific illegal activities. Yet, on the other hand, I can well imagine that he could have been seduced by the financial gains to be made.'

'Did you know for what purpose the properties he bought were used?'

'I most certainly did not and if they had been anything that I disapproved of I had I should have told him in no uncertain terms what I thought of him' her eyes sparkled with sudden anger.

'How much did you know about his financial affairs?'

'Virtually nothing .I have no idea where he banked or who was his accountant. He never once talked finance with me.'

'Thank you for your help Miss Oakes.'

'It is clear that Nigel was not a knight in shining armour Chief Superintendent, yet he could, on a personal level, be an interesting, amusing and generous friend.'

'What did you make of her sir?' asked Sparrow when they were back outside. 'I think she answered our questions pretty honestly. She is nobody's fool. I think it quite probable that she knew or guessed that her lover was not as innocent as he tried to make out but she simply did not want to know the gory details. He was a wealthy man who, in her own words, could be charming, amusing and generous. In the same way that she knew the relationship would not last she decided to enjoy its benefits whilst she could. Burgess seems to have worked on her like a snake charmer but I doubt if he ever pulled the wool entirely over her eyes. When she saw the end was coming, she simply accepted it on the basis that it had been nice whilst it lasted'

'Do you think she killed him sir?'

'You can never be dogmatic about people Sergeant. I have met the most unlikely people who have killed quite remorselessly. But, on what I know at present, she would not be my prime suspect. Apart from what one might think about her private morals I suspect that as far as business is concerned, she has moral scruples. A case of what you don't know can't harm you. It's just as well she has a solid alibi or she could have found herself in real trouble.'

'If you are crossing her off the list sir what are you going to do next?'

'I think I need to have a heart to heart with Mr Walter Legge and find out exactly what the lawyer did know about his clients' activities'

The offices of Parker, Jessup and Co. were situated in a Georgian property overlooking the Steyne in Brighton. Buxton waited outside until Sergeant Barnett had parked his car and then they entered through the glass panelled door. On their left was a glass window with a sign over it saying 'Enquiries'. Buxton pressed the bell on the shelf and shortly afterwards a young woman dressed in a neat black and white dress opened the window and greeted them with a smile.

'Can I help?' she asked in a well educated voice.
'Superintendent Buxton of the Sussex Police and this is Sergeant Barnett' the two men presented their credentials. 'We wish to speak with your senior partner please.'
'Do you have an appointment sir?'
'No but please tell him we are here.'
 Just one moment please.'

She closed the window and could be seen speaking on a telephone. Putting the receiver down she returned to the window, opened it and said,
'If you will go through those doors you will find the second door on the right leads into our conference room. Mr Jessup will join you there in a few moments. In the meantime, can I offer you tea or coffee?'
'Black coffee for me please' said Buxton, 'with one sugar.'
'White for me please,'   added Barnett 'with no sugar.'
They found their way into the conference room which was panelled in light oak and had a very long table down its centre. Along the table were a series of black folders by each of which there was a beer mat and a ball point pen. Each place had a green leather backed chair. When the door opened it was to admit the young lady with a tray of coffee and biscuits. She was followed by a man in a light grey suit, a blue shirt and red tie. He had short, fair hair and wore heavy tortoise shell glasses.
'Good morning gentlemen' he said with an ingratiating smile 'I am Paul Jessup the senior partner of this firm.'
'Chief Superintendent Buxton and this is Sergeant Barnett 'both men held out their identity cards 'We wish to obtain some information about the late Mr Nigel Burgess who I gather was a client of yours.'
'Yes indeed, 'replied Jessup 'please do sit down. This is a very sad business. Mr Burgess was a very valued client of this firm.' He opened the folder in front of his chair and took up the pen ready to make notes.

Buxton and Barnett seated themselves opposite him and Barnett followed his suit and opened his folder and, taking a pen from his pocket, made it clear that he too was going to record what was said.

'I believe that you agreed Mr Burgess's tax affairs with the authorities?' Buxton started his questions

'That is correct.'

'Did your firm also audit his accounts?'

'No, he preferred to keep his private affairs separate from the corporate ones.'

'Can you tell us what were the main sources of income that were included in his tax returns?'

'That is an easy question. 'smiled Mr Jessup 'they were, exclusively, income from his various companies. He held no investments such as stocks and shares or mutual funds and had no sums deposited with banks or building societies. He maintained that it was best to keep his tax return simple as it was the best way of avoiding problems with the Inland Revenue. His income was therefore his salary, bonus and dividends from the companies in which he held shares. Not all his companies actually paid dividends although, as I was careful to point out to him care was required to ensure that the Revenue did not claim that distributions should have been made and to seek to assess such notional distributions to tax.'

'Did he take advantage of any tax avoidance schemes sir? ' asked Barnett.

'Tax avoidance is a sensitive word Sergeant 'said Jessup 'I would prefer to use the description of tax mitigation. And, yes, Burgess did use certain of these. For example, we introduced Save As You Earn schemes in the major companies and share options.'

'Are you able to confirm that, in your opinion, Mr Burgess's tax returns showed he had sufficient disposable income to cover his lifestyle?' asked Buxton.

'Neither I nor the Inland Revenue had reason to think otherwise Chief Superintendent.

'Sufficient to cover the cost of the very large and expensive house he had built in Upper Burford?

'I assumed that he would have covered the cost by a mortgage.'

'Had you any reason to think that he had more cash at his disposal than his declared income would indicate?'

'Have you a reason for that question Chief Superintendent?'

Buxton looked at Barnett.

'Perhaps you would explain your uncertainty on this point Sergeant '

Barnett passed across the table to Paul Jessup apiece of paper on which was typed some letters and numbers.

'Do this mean anything to you Mr Jessup? he asked.

Jessup studied the paper for a minute or two before answering as if he was weighing his words before uttering them.

'Some time ago Mr Burgess asked me if I had any information about the operation of banking accounts in Switzerland. As you know gentlemen the Swiss banks offer a service of numbered accounts where the existence of the principal and the transactions are not revealed to any third party. I explained this to Nigel and asked him if he was thinking of using such an account. He laughed and said that if he ever did consider it, he would let me know. I never heard from him again on that topic. However, when we were talking, I jotted down some potential examples so he could see what I was talking about. The figures etc. on this paper look familiar and could be those I used as hypothetical examples. For instance, the first one uses the letters USB which I said could indicate United Swiss Bank if such a bank existed. The figures were an example of an account number. Another of these is ZIB or Zurich International Bank and this one HBG could be Hauptmann Brother of Geneva. They were all made up on the spur of the moment. As far as I know he did not open any such account and, quite frankly, if he did it is going to be very hard to get at it. You may have read the stories of the accounts supposedly held by Nazi leaders that have never been identified. 'he added with a laugh.
'I think that's all for the moment Mr Jessup 'Buxton got to his feet 'if we have further questions we will come and see you again.'

'What did you make of that Barnett?' Buxton asked when they were back in the street.
'Almost too good to be true sir. I will get onto checking put these SAYE Schemes and Share Options. They can be very good ways of making nice tax-free amounts and are used by most major companies.'
'What about the numbered account business? Did you buy what Jessup told us?'
'Only partly sir. I think it likely he did explain Swiss numbered account to Mr Burgess. However, as these initials and figures were in Burgess private papers, I would hazard a guess they refer to at least one real account. It would be a good way of washing the cash that Burgess had from his people smuggling and sex trade activities. Our next step is, I think, to compare the letters with a list of Swiss banks. My former employers have an office in Geneva and I think I might contact a friend who works there and see if he can throw any light on these letters.'
'Keep me posted please and do so directly and not through Inspector Love. Who is inclined to be myopic about this case.'
Meanwhile Inspector Underhill was following up the case of the man seen at Burgess' funeral. He was traced as the owner of a number of clubs and other properties in Manchester. His name was Mario Bellini and he originated from Sicily. He was questioned by a local police inspector.
'Do you know a Nigel Burgess sir?' asked the inspector.
'No, I have never heard the name.'

'Can you tell me where you were on the 3¹ May please?'
'I was here in Manchester attending to my business interests'
'The perhaps you can explain why your car was seen in West Sussex that afternoon?'
'I sometimes loan it to a friend.'
'Not only was your car seen in Sussex but you have been identified by a police officer as being with the car.'
'There is no law against being in Sussex.'
'Why did you go all that way to attend a funeral?'
'I did not attend any funeral. My car was delayed in a village by a funeral but I did not attend it.'
'Would it interest you to know that the funeral you did not attend was that of a Nigel Burgess?'
'Since I do not know this man it is of no interest to me.'
'We know that your business has had dealings with a company owned by Burgess so there is no point in denying that you know him. Where were you on 2 May this year?'
'I will check my diary' Bellini pulled out a slim volume 'yes, I was in Glasgow at the Continental Hotel.'
Subsequent investigation showed that he was indeed in Glasgow that day. Underhill thought it most probable that he had heard that Burgess was dead and wanted to make sure. It was quite possible he had paid for a shipment of girls but had not received delivery.

Finally, Underhill turned to Interpol to see if there was any information or rumour going the rounds along the Channel coast that suggested that a contract had been put out on the life of Nigel Burgess. As he expected this enquiry did not produce any direct evidence. Whoever had killed Burgess did not seem to be from the shadowy world of the sex trade and people smuggling.

CHAPTER 22

When he paid a second visit to see Walter Legge the Chief Superintendent was accompanied by Sergeant Barnett as he felt the sergeant's detailed knowledge of the corporate structure of the Burgess empire would be of assistance. Having taken the precaution of arranging an appointment in advance Buxton and Barnett were shown into a conference room furnished with a large walnut table and eight red leather dining chairs. The walls were papered in a regency stripe and had a number of lithograph prints of sailing boats on the walls.

'Good morning Chief Superintendent ' Walter Legge greeted Buxton with outstretched hand.' Good morning sir. May I introduce my colleague Sergeant Barnett.'
'Pleased to meet you sergeant. I gather you have been carrying out research into the late Nigel Burgess' business affairs.'
'Routine enquiries sir, ' replied Barnett.
'Since we last met Mr Legge the funeral has taken place so I assume that Mr Burgess' Will is now in what may be described as the public domain.'
'I agree that it is no longer necessary to treat that document as being privileged.'
'Are you able to let us know its principal provisions Mr Legge. I am sure that you will understand that information contained in that document could be of help to us in our enquiries.'
'Whilst what you say may be the case in certain instances Chief Superintendent, I am not sure the contents of the Will are going to be of much help to you.'
'Perhaps you could summarise them for us Mr Legge.'
'The Will appoints the National and Southern Bank and myself as executors and trustees. To be perfectly honest I could see no real need to involve the bank. However, Nigel was adamant he wanted them appointed. Personally, I think it was because the local manager was a frequent golf partner. I have nothing against bank trustee departments but they do tend to be somewhat hidebound and pedantic in their business methods. It was because of that fact that I persuaded Nigel to appoint me as co-executor.'
'You will understand if Sergeant Barnett makes some notes Mr Legge .' said Buxton ' please go on.'
'Nigel Burgess' shares in Burgess Homes are to be offered to the other directors on a pro rata basis. Each of the directors has agreed to make similar dispositions as it ensures the control of that business has continuity. After the usual payment of funeral and other debts there are a number of pecuniary legacies that amount to some twenty thousand pounds.'
'May I ask who were the legatees?'
'They were one or two local charities, his secretary gets two thousand pounds and I am to receive five thousand pounds in recognition of our long standing business relationship the rest, as I say goes to local charities. The residue of the

estate, after payment of debts and expenses is divided between five nationally known charities. Nothing particularly special about any of this.'
'Have you any idea as to the size of the estate?'
'Full details are not yet to hand Chief Superintendent but I imagine that the net estate will be in the region of three quarters of a million pounds plus.'
'In most circumstances that would be a tempting target 'said Buxton
'But hardly true in this case where the main beneficiaries are charities.'
'Am I correct in thinking that your firm provided legal services to Mr Burgess' business interests as well as being his personal legal representative?'
'You are quite correct Chief Superintendent.'
'This would include his buy to let companies?'
'It would.'
'As well acting in any purchase or sale would your firm draft leases for the properties to be let?'
'Unless they were what may be called short term lettings then that would be the case.'
Buxton looked across at Barnett who said,
'I think it is usual in most leases and agreements for the tenant to agree that the property should not be used for illegal or immoral purposes?'
'That is indeed a standard condition in a lease.'
'Would it surprise you to know that in some cases the leases for Mr Burgess' properties did not contain that covenant?'
'If the lease did not do so then it must have been because of the wishes of the landlord.'
'You would not find that omission irregular Mr Legge? 'asked Buxton.
'We would be providing a service to our client and would naturally follow his instructions as long as they did not infringe the law.'
'In that case would you be surprised to find that when this happened the property was being used for one of the usually restricted purposes.'
'If it was then the landlord would be placing himself at risk.'
'Please tell Mr Legge, sergeant, the use to which these properties were put.'
'They were used as what are known as Massage Parlours where it is hard to differentiate the services provided to those of a brothel.'
'I had no idea this was the case I assure you.' blustered Legge who was looking increasingly uncomfortable.
'In drawing up the lease presumably it is the landlord who sets the rent?'
'That is correct.'
'So, the fact that the rent may be way over what may be seen as the market rate for that type of property for a residential letting would not cause any problem ?'
'As I say it is the landlord who sets the rent. The ongoing management would be handled by the appropriate Burgess company.'
'When Mr Burgess wished to set up a company in Jersey, did he come to you for assistance sir?'

Legge looked taken back by the sudden change of tack in the questioning.
'He did ask what we could do and I directed him to our agent firm in St Hellier. Beyond that we had no involvement in the formation of the company.'
'Did Mr Burgess tell you why he wanted a Jersey based company?'
'He was fond of sailing I knew and I gathered that he planned to have a boat based in the Channel Islands.'
'Did he say what type of boat he had in mind Mr Legge ?'
'I seem to recollect that he had a fishing boat in mind as he could use it both for pleasure and for business.'
'Did he tell you that the business he had in mind was people smuggling?'
Again, Legge looked worried but recovered quickly.
'He most certainly did not. To be frank I find it hard to believe that he did what you are alleging.'
'I can assure you that he did sir, 'said Barnett. 'The authorities have a number of people in custody arising from charges of people smuggling including supplying young women to so called massage parlours. All of which transactions used the boat owned by Mr Burgess' company'
'As I have said I had no knowledge of the kind of business you are mentioning.'
'It seems Mr Legge as though your client was engaged in a number of highly irregular if not downright illegal activities for which he used companies created for or on behalf of your firm.' said Buxton.
'Come now Chief Superintendent because a client asks me to carry out a perfectly ordinary legal transaction such as forming a limited company it does not mean that I am in any way responsible for how he operated that legal entity.'
'Is it correct that all these companies give this address as their registered office?'
'Again, that is a quite usual arrangement. If you care to look at the list of companies on the notice boards on our ground floor you will see that this is the case not only for Nigel Burgess but for many other clients.'
'According to the information held by Companies House sir, 'said Barnett 'you are named a Secretary for all the companies you formed for Mr Burgess.'
'I am sure you are quite well aware Sergeant that this again is quite a normal arrangement. People who form companies are not always the most efficient in ensuring that all the statutory information is lodged on the due date and they employ their solicitor to act as Secretary to ensure that there are no problems in that direction.'
'So, you would sum up your business arrangements with Mr Burgess as being entirely in line with the normal run of services provided by a firm of solicitors?'
'I couldn't put it better myself Chief Superintendent.'
'And how your client operated those companies was not in your remit?'
'Exactly.'

'Well thank you very much for your help Mr Legge. I think that is all our questions at the moment. We will leave the question of the implication arising from the fees paid to you personally as Secretary to these companies for another day.'

Before the solicitor could reply Buxton stood up and he and Barnett left the room.

'Talk about see no evil, hear no evil and speak no evil 'Barnett said as they left the building.
'My thoughts exactly Sergeant. I think we have given our friend Mr Legge enough to think about for one day.'
'Do you think there are any charges we could lay against him sir?'
'I rather doubt it. He may have sailed close to the wind but I suspect that he has been careful not to break any laws. It may be that the Law Society will want to ask their own questions. As indeed may his partners in that law firm. One way or another I think our Mr Legge is in for an uncomfortable time.'

When the chief superintendent updated the Assistant Chief Constable on his interviews with Burgess' accountant and lawyer there followed a fairly lengthy discussion as to what additional information could be uncovered that might give a lead to the person who had killed the businessman.

'There seem to me to be two lines of enquiry that we need to follow up sir, 'said Buxton.
'One for each of the Burgess and the Hope cases. We believe that Burgess had money deposited in numbered Swiss bank accounts. If we get information about the transactions in those accounts we might possibly get a line on some new business interest that we have not yet uncovered. As far as the Hope case is concerned there is the mystery as to whether or not she was in contact with Herr Schneider when he was in England during the war. It would be useful to know a bit more about that gentleman and his wartime activities.'
'In other words, you would not mind a trip to Zurich 'laughed the ACC.
'It's not that I want to go there sir, it's just that I think we may get some useful information.'
'Very well I will have a word with the Chief to get his approval. '

'Here's Mr Craigton to see you father' said Brenda.

'How are you today Arnold? 'asked Donald Craigton.

'Could be worse or could be better Mr Craigton' said the old man with a grin.

'In other words, there is no point in complaining.'

'I have brought you some Sussex County magazines that I hope will help pass the time.'

'That's very good of you. I get tired of watching the same old things on the television. I always did like a good read.'

Having made himself comfortable in the chair offered to him Donald introduced the topic that had brought him to visit Arnold Treacher.

When I saw you last you told me some fascinating things about life in the village before and at the start of the war, before you were called up. I have been thinking about what you said and I believe it is important that there is a record of those days for future generations. Do you think you would be up to writing down your memories? I could then see that they are stored among the parish records.'

'I was never one for writing Mr Craigton I am not sure that I could do what you ask, especially with this arthritis in my hands these days.'

'How about if we talk about them and I make some notes and put them into a proper shape that you could read and say whether I have got the facts right.'

'I think I could manage to talk alright' the old man laughed 'my wife always said I could talk the hind leg off a donkey.'

'What I suggest is that if we agree a subject then you could give it some thought and, when I came to see you next, we could talk it over and I will take notes and write them up. Do you think that would work?'

'I think it is a very good idea. There is nothing wrong with my memory thank the Lord.'

'How about if we start with what happened in nineteen forty. You just talk away and I will make notes in this notebook. If I am not clear about anything I can I ask a question. Is that alright with you?'

'Sound s fine to me. Where did you want me to start?'

'How about what happened after Dunkirk ?'

For the next hour Arnold spoke about those days of over forty years ago. From time to time Donald asked a question or pointed him in a certain direction. At the end of the hour Donald called a halt.

'That should be enough for today Arnold. I don't want Brenda after me for tiring you out 'Donald said closing his notebook.
'You know Mr Craigton I never realised quite how much I do remember from that long ago.
'You certainly have a good memory Arnold. Tell me how many of those people you have mentioned are still with us?'
'Not so many. A lot of them were older than me and have been long gone. Some of them are on the war memorial and some have moved away so I don't know what happened to them. I reckon its only the younger ones who are still alive. I am a bit of an ancient mariner in that regard 'he laughed.
'Can you give me some names Arnold?'
'Well there's Wilfred Main and Tommy Gordon and Sam Newton. They are still alive and kicking and I see them at the war memorial on 11th November. Harry Thorne and Gordon Hanley and Fred Howlett are all on the war memorial. They never made it back home. Apart from those there is only young Megan Legge who rode her horse to collect messages though she's not as spry as she used to be.'
'I think you said she was away during the war. Do you know where?'
'Sorry but I don't have the foggiest. I think she went to London. She had been to school in France you know so perhaps they wanted her for work involving that language. She has never said and I have never asked. Must have been something because she is always at the war memorial and come to think of it, she has a couple of war medals so she must have joined up at some stage.'
'Did many of the local girls do that?'
'Quite a few. They saw it as a chance to get away from being in service and of avoiding working in a factory in Portsmouth. I recall Eileen Dennis and Gladys Knott were in the WRNS and Kate Young was in the WAAF. My misses, bless her, was in the ATS. That's where I met her.'
'Well thank you very much Arnold I will see what I can do to get this written out and then I will let you have a copy to check that I have got down correctly.'

Over the next few days Donald Craigton, as part of his duties as curate at the local church, made it his business to talk to Arnold several times and to make enquiries about those residents who recalled what life was like during the second world war. He gave as his excuse the fact that the following year would be the fortieth anniversary of the end of the war and he was considering how the village might recognise that fact and celebrate the lives of those who had served their country during those six years.   In fact, he was planning to produce a booklet that would put these memories on record for future generations. He found that the men he talked to had differing views on the war. Some felt that having had to go through shot and shell and having seen their friends blown to pieces all they wanted was to forget and trust that no new generation would have to go through the same experience. Others had however felt that they had been an active part of the fight against Nazism and their contribution should be remembered by younger people. As far as the women were concerned most of those who had been in the forces said it was the best years of their lives especially when the GIs arrived with nylon stockings and plenty of cigarettes. The women who had worked on the land remembered it as being a time of hard work in often terrible conditions. Yet, for nearly all the women it had been a time of liberation from household chores.

Having spoken to those who had been adults in the forties he turned to those who were ten or more years younger at the time to see if they had any memories. One man he spoke to recalled that, as a Boy Scout, he had helped with air raid practices by being a "patient" and being put on a stretcher into the back of a lorry. He remembered also that his brother, who was a bit older, had in the very early days, stood guard on the railway line. One of the women remembered how, after the war, when she was a Guide they had been on a hike when they saw some men coming down by parachute and had asked the Guider, as a joke, if she had ever done a parachute jump. When she said that she had jumped with a parachute from a balloon they all laughed at the idea of her jumping from anything higher than a wooden stile.

'If you saw he now you would laugh even louder,' the woman said 'she's put on a lot of weight since those days.'

  It might be interesting, Craigton thought, to see what comments there were, if any, in books and records relating to the war period that mentioned the village by name.

CHAPTER 24

It was Inspector Thomasson's first visit to Liverpool. The Assistant Chief
Constable had spoken to his colleague in the city and had been assured that the
local force would do all they could to help their visitor. When Thomasson
alighted from the train and made his way to the barrier, he saw a uniformed
police officer standing a little way back. As he approached him the officer held
out a hand.
'Inspector Thomasson? I am Inspector Frank Youngman of the City Police.
Welcome to Liverpool.'
Thomasson took the offered hand and confirmed his identity.
'Your first visit to the city?'
'Yes. I have visited the Lake District a number of times but never Liverpool.'
'I gather from our ACC that you are interested in one of our residents.'
'That's correct.'
'Well let's go and find a cup of coffee and you can tell me who he is and what
your interest is in him.'

They made their way out of the station and into a nearby coffee bar. Seated at
an isolated table with cups of coffee and French pastries. Thomassons's gave
his colleague details of the Audrey Hope case.
 Something of an old battle axe by the sound of it ' Yeoman grinned ' but hardly
enough to make someone want to top her nor why you have come all the way
from the south coast.'
'What I didn't mention was that she was a pretty extreme right-wing Tory'
 If that were a motive for murder, we both would be rushed off our feet.'
 'Agreed but while she was teaching there was a young man who joined the
staff, just down from university, who was as far left wing as she was right wing.
Needless to say, they did not see eye to eye. It seems it got so bad that the head
teacher had to ban politics in the staff room. The young man whose name was
Grant Cooper was a member of something called the Army of the Republican
Proletariat whose policy was, as far as I can understand it, to overthrow all
vestiges of society as it exists today, including the monarchy, and introduce a
workers if not an anarchist's paradise.'
 Rings a bell or two' said Youngman.' This city seems to attract some of the
more esoteric political theorists.'
'It seems that young Cooper stood for the local council and in the general
election and only managed to accumulate a very small vote so much so that he
lost his deposit. It so happened that our deceased was at the count as a
representative of the Conservatives. Cooper, no doubt realising his poor
performance, had been drowning his sorrows. His speech on the announcement
of the result was pretty inflammatory and some people wanted the Returning

Officer to throw him out. Before he left, he buttonholed our deceased and told
her that one day the gutters would run with her blood.'
'That didn't go down well I'll bet.'
 'It was brushed aside as the ramblings of a drunk and forgotten. Cooper left the
school at once and moved to Liverpool. Among the deceased's papers we found
several leaflets from this APR that must have been posted to her. Why she had
kept them we have no idea. However, in all the circumstances our people
thought it would be a good idea to have a quiet word with Mr Cooper and
ascertain where he was on the day of the murder.'
'That seems reasonable in all the circumstances. Do you have an address for
him?'
'All we know is that he obtained a post as a lecturer in physics at the Frederick
Vernon University. We have checked with the latest University Yearbook and it
seems he is still on the staff.'
 Then let's make our way over there. I have a car standing by. I will just call it
up.'

On arrival at the university they sought out the Dean of Studies and asked if
they could see Grant Cooper.

'Oh dear' sighed The Dean,' has been getting himself into trouble again?'
'Not that we are aware of 'replied Yeoman. 'However, my colleague here
would like to ask him some questions to assist him in certain enquiries with
which he is concerned.'
'Then I had better check to see if he is on site.'

 He rang a number on an internal phone and was told that Dr Cooper was in the
university and could be found in his room. After consulting an internal
telephone directory, the Bursar dialled a number.
"Dr Cooper? It is the Dean of Studies here. Are you able to come to my office
please? There are some gentlemen who would like a few words with you.'

'The voice at the other end said something and the Dean replied;
 I think it easier if I left them to explain the reason for their visit.' He put down
the receiver. 'He should be here in a few minutes and you can use the adjoining
conference room.'
The man who entered the Dean's office was in his late thirties. He had long
brown hair that almost reached his shoulders, had a grizzled beard and grey eyes
behind rimless spectacles. He was wearing a faded sweatshirt with the motto
Change is Coming, baggy corduroy trousers and scuffed tan coloured boots.
'Dr Cooper this is Inspector Yeoman of the City Police and Inspector
Thomasson of the Sussex Police. They are seeking your assistance.'
'I have nothing to say to these agents of fascist oppression.'

'Dr Cooper, " snapped the Dean ' may I remind you that you are on University grounds and that therefore you are expected to treat visitors with normal courtesy. I suggest you use the conference room through there.'
'If they want to talk to me let them produce a warrant.'
'Dr Cooper may I remind you who I am and the position I hold in this University. May I also remind you that your tenure here will be up for review shortly. Kindly do as you have been requested and show some common courtesy. If you are asked questions you do not wish to answer the you are free to tell these gentlemen so.'
With this he got to his feet and opened a door and ushered the two officers and Dr Cooper into the conference room.'
'Inspector Thomasson has some questions he wishes to ask you relating to an inquiry he is conducting.'
'Dr Cooper' said Thomasson 'does the name Audrey Hope mean anything to you?'
'No'
'You were a teacher at a college in Portsmouth some year ago?'
'Yes.'
'Then you will recall that Miss Hope was the head of the modern language department at that school'
'You mean the fascist female? Was that her name?'
'Did you stand for parliament at the general election as a candidate for the Army of the Proletarian Republic ?'
'Possibly. That is not yet a crime in this police state is it?'
'You were not elected?'
'Our time will come then you will see what a free society is all about.'
'We have witnesses that at the count you spoke to Miss Hope who was there as a representative of another party.'
'What if I did?'
'You told her that in due time the gutters would run with her blood.'
'Come the proletariat revolution the fascists will have to pay for their crimes.'
 Did you have any contact with Miss Hope after that date?'
'I shook the dirt of Hampshire off my feet and came to where people believe in the power of the proletariat.'
'In that case how is it that in the deceased's papers we found half a dozen leaflets published by the Army of the Proletarian Republic?
'How should I know? Our administration people must have had her name and address and sent her our publications to educate her.'
'Then you may be interested to know that Miss Hope has been murdered.'
'You're not expecting me to subscribe for a wreath are you? If so, you have wasted your time and the tax payer's money.'
' Where were you on the evening of 12th May? 'asked Yeoman.
'That's a good one 'snorted Cooper.

'What do you mean?'

'I mean that you, of all people, should know where I was.'

Please answer the question Dr Cooper.'

If you must know I was incarcerated in one of your cells. '

On what charge?'

'I was falsely accused of being drunk and disorderly. I certainly was not in Hampshire or wherever killing that fascist old woman took place.'

With that Dr Cooper got to his feet and walked out.

CHAPTER 25

Donald Craigton decided to host a tea party at which he hoped to get reaction to the idea of a booklet telling the story of the village at war. He invited the people who made up the informal group that met at The Six Bells plus Walter and Megan Legge, Verity Trumper as well as one or two of the more elderly residents who had given him information and he went and fetched Arnold Treacher. Once everyone was seated in the large lounge and Harold Whitehouse had performed the duties of waiter Donald began to explain the reason for the meeting.

'It all started when I was talking to Arnold about life in the village in past years. He told me a lot of interesting stories about the nineteen thirties and then touched on what happened during the war, especially in 1940 when there was a threat of invasion. This led me to have the idea that, as next year will be the fortieth anniversary of VE Day, it might be interesting to produce a small booklet about life in the village and the lives of villagers during that time. I have let each of you have a chance to read what I have learned and now I am hoping that you will tell me if I am painting an accurate picture. '
'Is this to be a profit making enterprise?' asked Verity Trumper.
'Not at all. If there is any money made out of selling the booklets, I am proposing that it is paid to British Legion. Now please do let me have your comments and ideas as to how it could be improved.'
'I think' said Mrs Helen Green one of the elderly ladies 'that some more could be said about food rationing and how the village responded with things like allotments and a pig club.'
'What was a pig club? 'asked Olga Sanderson.
'A number of people kept a pig and when it was killed, they shared the meat among the members of the club.'
'I know food was tight' said Olivia 'but being in ENSA we tended to get fed. Mind you they had our ration books.'
'What about the issue of gas masks 'said Robert Little one of the older men 'and the role of the ARP and the fire watchers.'
'If you will let me have more comments on those points I can include them', said Donald. 'Perhaps you could jot them down on a piece of paper for me.'
'What about you Walter' asked Trevor Nightingale 'what did you do ?'
'I was called up and posted to the Adjutant General's Office to deal with a whole range of legal matters from conscientious objectors to dealing with the legal side of properties that were taken over by the government. I was only in the village when I was on leave so I am afraid there is not much I can add to this story.'
'And what about you Megan?' asked Olga. 'What did you do?'

'To start with I was a sort of messenger for the Home Guard because I had a horse and a bicycle. However, that was only short termed. By the time I was twenty-one I was called up. I was posted to the War Office because I spoke French having been to school in that country. I spent my time doing various things arising from our contacts with the Free French. Nothing that warrants a mention in any book.'

'Where were you during the war Verity? 'asked Trevor Nightingale.

'I was at a boarding school that was evacuated to the Welsh countryside. In one sense we had a very sheltered war. We were not subject to bombs or VI or V2 rockets. Apart from the fact that some girls would get information that their father or brother was missing or killed the war had little effect on us. My father's diocese was a rural one so there was little to see about war when I went home for a holiday.'

'Were there evacuees here? 'asked Donald.

'A few came in 1939 'said Helen Green' but they went back to London and then with the threat of invasion they did not send any more. We were still subject to air raids and a few doodlebugs right through until well after D-Day so there were few strangers in the village.'

At this point Harold reappeared to refill tea cups and pass round more sandwiches and cakes and the conversation became general.

'One final question 'said Donald. 'Do you think its worthwhile printing a small booklet like this?'

'Yes 'said Arnold Treacher ' I think it's important the young people are given a chance to know what happened during those years. It's probably the best way to make sure no future generation has to go through the same thing. War is a terrible thing as anyone who had to fight in it will tell you. Those of us who did saw things and went through things we would never wish anyone else to see or experience.'

'Quite right Mr Treacher' said Megan Legge. 'The damage and deaths in London and other places were dreadful. The fact that this village escaped all that does not mean that people should think people who came from here did not suffer in different ways.'

' Then, when I have your further comments, I will produce a final draft 'said Donald. 'Thank you for sparing the time to come along this afternoon.'

Later, when he had received the extra notes, he had asked for Craigton edited his draft of the notebook and read it through. All in all, he felt it painted a reasonable picture of Upper Burford in wartime. There was just the one point that had been troubling him for some time. There was a fact secreted there that hid something important. He reached out and telephoned his friend in Oxford with a question that had suddenly become clear to him. At the end of the conversation he replaced the phone and began to consider a most disturbing chain of thought.

CHAPTER 26

Tell me Harold, 'Craigton asked his butler cum housekeeper 'when you were in the RAF did you ever come across anyone who had any connection with the secret services? '

'There was an officer my lord who used to like to tell stories in the Mess of how he had both dropped off and picked up our agents in occupied France. He used to fly a small plane called a Lysander I believe. The other thing he boasted about was that he was a member of an exclusive club called The Special Forces in Europe.'

'Did he say where this club was situated?'

'He claimed it was in Pall Mall right in the centre of what used to be called club land.'

'Did you, in your previous existence, ever enter any of these hallowed halls?'

'I have had occasion, my lord, to enter both the Reform Club and the Athenaeum.'

'Which is more than I ever did in my former existence' laughed Craigton.

He raised the topic of life in the village during the war one morning to the usual group in The Six Bells. Trevor Nightingale said that as he had been born in 1939, he had no memories of the war especially as his family had lived on a farm in the remotest part of Cornwall.

Norman Alkham, who was now about sixty years old said that he had been called up and drafted as a Bevin Boy and had to spend three years down a coal mine in Kent. Olga told him about being a dancer with the Ballet and that her memories of the war were of hard work and having to perform in all sorts of outrageous places that had never had a ballet performance within a hundred miles before. Besides the disciplines that the young dancers were placed under, by Madam were so strict that her only memories were of travelling in unheated trains, terrible lodgings and being exhausted from rehearsals and performances. 'It was not exactly the life of a modern-day celebrity 'she laughed.

'I spent the first part of the war,' said Olivia 'singing with various bands in night clubs. Then, in 1941, I was invited to join ENSA to help entertain the troops. From then on, I was part of various touring groups who gave concerts to troops and to factory workers. In 1944 I went over to France with a group to entertain the troops fighting their way towards Germany. This involved appearing in chateaux and on the back of lorries as well as in orchards and aircraft hangers. At various times I was bombed and doodle bugged and shot up by German planes. Yet we always had to be bright and cheerful, be dressed in our finery and look as if we were enjoying ourselves. I met and performed with some famous and very nice stars as well as some lovely other people. Even if there were some who would have struggled to get into their local amateur

Gilbert and Sullivan Society'

Craigton used all the information he had gathered to make a start on drafting the sort of booklet that he had in mind. When he had completed this work and read through his draft, he decided that what it lacked if only in a negative sense was any information about the village and its inhabitants in the wider picture of the war.   Whilst mulling this over he found that one particular piece of information he had been given kept creeping into the back his mind. What it meant he did not know and he decided that if he left it alone it would either go away or would reveal itself more clearly. He thought it was something to do with what he had suggested to Richard Buxton. The solution to his enquiry might well be connected to something that happened a long time ago.

He was due to take a few days holiday so he told Harold he was free to do the same.

'What do you propose to do Harold?' he asked.
'I thought I might take a trip to Lindesfarne, my lord. It's a place I have often wished to visit.'
'A very interesting and beautiful place.'
'And you my lord ? Have you anywhere in mind ?'
'I think I will go to London.' replied Craigton 'and do some research in the Libraries and Museums.'

Before he left Craigton got out his old address book and looked up a particular acquaintance. When he was studying to be a Licensed Reader, he had met a man following similar studies, who was an historian and had been employed by several authors who were doing research on books being written by leading historians. He had also worked on authorised histories published by various government departments. It was through him that Craigton had obtained access to the British Museum Reading Room and the Imperial War Museum. Fortunately his friend was still at the same Oxford college and was delighted to learn that Craigton had taken holy orders. They arranged to meet for lunch at an Italian Restaurant that Craigton had frequented when he was based in London. Over good food and excellent wine they exchanged their news. Craigton told his friend about his efforts to write a brief history of his village during the war and how he had received hints that one or more of the residents might have been attached to one the secret services. Was it possible to see if this was fact or fiction. His friend gave him the names of several publications which might contain information. In addition, he identified some books and papers that might contain reference to Upper Burford.

'Have you ever heard of the Special Forces in Europe Club? Craigton asked.

'I came across it when I was working on a SOE report on its French activities. Why?'
 It was mentioned to me in passing. Is it possible for someone like me to get into a place like that?
'Generally speaking, I would say no, but your luck is in.'
'What do you mean ?'
'When I was working on that SOE report I was given a membership card which I still have. I am not in London that much but, from time to time, I drop into the club for a pint and a natter. Would you like to see it?'
'I would indeed.'

The club was in an imposing, if small, building. Craigton was signed in and shown over the premises. He was also able to look through the list of members to see if any of them came from his village. He was interested to see the name of Arnold Treacher and wondered if the old man had ever visited the place. He was interested also to see other local names that he recognised. Additionally, he was given several pamphlets that set out the aims and objectives of the club and the type of activities covered by its members. In addition, he was provided with the titles of some books that might be of interest to him. It had proved an interesting and helpful afternoon.

Over the next three days Craigton visited the Imperial War Museum and the British Museum and consulted the books that had been mentioned to him which added a great deal to his understanding of the secret war that had been waged by Britain during the dark years of the war. Although he did not find any specific mention of Upper Burford in anything he read he did find reference to people whom he had no idea had been part of the secret war. When he got back home, he telephoned his friend in Oxford to thank him for his help. He took the opportunity to ask him some supplementary questions which threw additional light on to what he had learned. Having incorporated what he felt able to do into his draft booklet he sat back and considered what he had learned. One thing was clear namely that there were local people who had not spoken about what they had done during the war. This was not surprising because, as was clear from the Bletchley Park revelations, that generation had taken the signing of the Official Secrets Act very seriously. His next thought was about the extent he may have been right in saying to Richard Buxton that the cause of the village murder could lie quite a way in the past. The problem with that was that Nigel Burgess was no more than a child during the war years so it was virtually impossible to think that his death was in any way related to events that happened that long ago. He wasn't so certain however if this applied to the other death the police were investigating.

CHAPTER 27

When Buxton emerged from the arrival area at Zurich airport there was someone holding a card with the name "Richard Buxton" printed on it. He introduced himself to the man who appeared to be a chauffeur as he was dressed in a dark suit, a white shirt and dark blue tie and well-polished black shoes. 'Welcome to Zurich sir ' the man said in good English ' my name is Heron and I am attached to the Embassy in Berne. I have a car waiting outside to take you to the Consulate.'

Buxton, who had never visited Zurich before looked with interest at the buildings and people that they passed and was impressed at how ordered and tidy everything was compared to other big cities such as London and Paris. The car drew into the driveway of a large house which carried a sign at the entrance announcing it was the British Consulate.

'I think you will find that Mr Denton, the Commercial Secretary at the Embassy is expecting you.'

At the reception area Buxton introduced himself and produced his credentials. A young woman dressed in a black skirt and red blouse escorted him to an upper floor and knocked on a door, opened it and announced;

'Chief Superintendent Buxton, Mr Denton'

The room was large and behind a desk sat a man in his late thirties wearing a dark grey suit, a light blue shirt and a striped tie such as worn by most public school pupils. He got to his feet and held out a hand.

'Pleased to meet you Chief Superintendent. My name is Gerald Denton. Take a pew while I order up some coffee.'

Buxton sat in the comfortable chair facing the desk.

'Now then, 'said Gerald Denton having given instructions over the internal telephone for coffee and pastries 'I gather you are here in connection with some inquiries you are engaged on back in the UK'

'That's correct Mr Denton. We are investigating two murders where both victims appear to have had some connection with Zurich. I am hoping you might be able to give me some assistance with regard to one of them. My enquiries relating to the other will involve contact with Interpol and I am in touch with them about that. The first case relates to a businessman in forties who was stabbed to death in his own back garden. I don't think he expected to go so young because he made no real effort to tidy up his financial affairs. On the face of it he was a very successful estate agent and property owner cum developer. Underneath those headings we have found that he was involved in the sex industry and in people smuggling. Our enquiries have led us to believe that he probably had some numbered accounts with a bank or banks here in

Zurich. Unfortunately, we have not been able to find anything by way of firm evidence apart from a note of what we are led to believe are letters identifying some local banks and some figures which an accountant tells us could well be those of numbered accounts. This is where I hope that your knowledge of the Swiss banking system might be of assistance.'

At this point the door opened and a young man brought in a tray with a coffee pot and some cups together with a plate on which were laid out some delicious looking pastries. Having served the coffee and pastries Denton picked up the story.

'As I am sure you will know Chief Superintendent the Swiss banks guard client confidentiality very tightly. As a general rule they just do not disclose information to anyone.'

'What I want to know is whether the information we have is correct. In other words, did the deceased have such an account. I would also like to know when it was opened and how much is held in it. It is quite possible that such information could lead us to the killer. I appreciate that it will be a matter for the executors to deal with the closure of the account. In addition, it would be helpful to know if he had any safe deposit with the bank and, if so, what it contains.'

'What information do you actually have about the existence of such accounts ?'

Buxton opened his briefcase and took out a file from which he extracted a piece of paper which he passed across the desk.

'Do you think this information does relate to bank accounts?'

Denton studied the piece of paper carefully.

'Do you think he had money with all these banks?'

'I don't know but its possible he had an account with only one or two. Some of this information comes from his accountant who told him about these accounts but had no part in opening any of them. The information in front of you was found in a safe in the deceased's property.'

'Well there are three sets of initials here that do indicate a bank. UIZ is the Union International of Zurich; HPIB is Huber and Partners International Bank and KSB is the Klaus Schroeder Bank. To be quite frank I am not sure that if you simply ask them if they have an account for the deceased person, that they will tell you. If you tell them you know the account number and the account holder and the reason for your enquiry you may be slightly more fortunate but I wouldn't put my shirt on it.'

'As this is a police investigation I thought it best to contact the local police and I have arranged that Police Commissioner Frei will accompany me when I call on the banks. If you were able to come along as well it might just be enough to get us the basic information I need.'

'I have met Commissioner Frei and if anyone can get information out of these banks it is him. It will be an education to come along with you.'

Commissioner Frei proved to be a tall man with very short steel grey hair, grey piercing eyes and a military moustache. He was wearing his official uniform. He spoke some English so its was very useful to have Gerald Denton to act as an interpreter. After introductions Buxton explained the reason for his visit. He emphasised that he believed that the money in these accounts came from criminal activities. He conceded that he did not expect to obtain full information about the accounts but it would help his investigation if he could discover when the account was opened and how monies were paid into to it as well as if there had been any withdrawals. As far as credits were concerned, he would like to know where they came from. Finally, he would like to know if the bank held anything in a safe custody box for Nigel Burgess. What followed was a mixture of a disinclination to tell him anything and the skill of Commissioner Frei in eliciting the facts that lay behind the numbered accounts. In every case the bank said that Burgess has signed a statement that the funds to be deposited were not the proceeds of a crime. To this Commissioner Frei retorted that Burgess may not have seen people smuggling as a crime but it was most certainly illegal. Eventually it was accepted by each of the banks that they did have a numbered account for Nigel Burgess. Buxton was able to produce a copy of the death certificate and proof of his own position in the British police force. The banks, after pressure from Frei and Denton revealed that the accounts had been opened personally by Burgess and that all credits had been received in the form of cash which, again, was deposited by Burgess himself. The current balances on these accounts totalled 450,000 Swiss Francs. In two instances Burgess also held a safe deposit box with the bank. It was only after lengthy negotiations and reference to the bank head offices that the visitors were allowed to see the boxes opened. Each held a small leather bag which contained what looked like stones. Commissioner Frei was quick to identify these as uncut diamonds. The banks said they were unaware of the contents which had been deposited by Burgess personally.

It was as much as Buxton could have hoped for given the strict privacy rules applied by the banks and he was certain that he would not have got that much information if it had not been for the combined efforts of Commissioner Frei and Gerald Denton. Having expressed his thanks to both of them Buxton booked into his hotel. His next appointment was not until the following day so he spent the time reviewing what he had learned and how that information fitted in with the picture that was being drawn of why Nigel Burgess had been killed. There was little doubt that the money and other valuables held in Switzerland came from people smuggling which had proved a very profitable business for Burgess. If it was that profitable it was possible that other people wanted to get in on the act and that, in itself, could have led to someone deciding that the best way to get their hands on to the trade handled by Burgess was to have him removed. When he got back to the UK, he would get Bill Underhill to make enquiries to see if there was any evidence that there were new players in what had previously been Burgess's field of operations. If there were then it would be necessary to see whether any of them could have been behind the killing. In the meanwhile, he set his mind to consider what he hoped he might learn from the next day's meeting with Interpol.

The meeting with Commandant Laurence Bourges took place at the Interpol office in Zurich. The Commandant was a man in his early forties, tall and slim with fair hair and blue eyes. He was wearing a well styled light grey suit, a pale pink shirt and a red tie. He welcomed Buxton into his office and it became clear that he spoke excellent English. When he had arranged his visit, Buxton had provided Interpol with the reasons why he was seeking their help.

'I am investigating the murder of an unmarried English woman in her sixties who had close ties with Zurich going back to the nineteen thirties. 'he said after the usual formalities had been dealt with.' She came here as a young woman and, among the various jobs she did, was to teach English to the young son of a Swiss family. She returned to the United Kingdom at the start of the war and was employed by the British government in its Foreign Ministry where her knowledge of German was a useful asset. We have found out that the Swiss man who employed her to tutor his son was in London as a Commercial Attaché at the Swiss embassy from 1942 to 1944.The woman, whose name was Audrey Hope, never said that she knew this man was in London or whether or not she had any contact with him. After the war Audrey Hope became a school teacher and visited Switzerland and in particular this area every year. She had a real affection for the country, its people and its way of life. In addition to all this we have learned that she held strong right wing views. What I would like to try and find out is whether the name Herr Dr Heinrich Schneider rings any bells with the Swiss authorities. That Audrey Hope maintained contact with the family is confirmed by the fact that his son attended her funeral.'

'You are trying to find out if this lady did have contact with a Swiss diplomat whilst working for the British secret services. Switzerland was a neutral country during the war. That does not mean that all Swiss people were strictly neutral. This has been something of a problem for the Swiss authorities and there have been reports that certain people were in fact pro-Nazi and may well have passed on information to the Germans. There is no doubt that this country was a great place for spying by one side or the other. A number of journalists have written articles and reports on this and some have pointed the finger at Swiss nationals. We have copies of the most important of these publications and I suggest that we take a look at them to see if they tell us anything about Herr Dr Schneider. He picked up the internal phone and gave some instructions in French. Shortly

afterwards a young woman knocked at the door and brought in a number of folders which she placed on the desk.'
'I think I will ask our records if they have anything on this man Schneider.' There followed another phone call during which Commandant Bourges wrote down a number of notes.
'Well it seems that the family firm of this Dr Schneider was involved in the chemical industry and did quite a lot of business with both Germany and Britain. He was obviously a natural choice for the position of Commercial Attaché at the embassy in London. He married a Fraulein Gerda Hess who was of German birth and a distant relation of a certain Rudolph Hess. The minister in Bern, who was responsible for appointing Herr Schneider, was a Herr Rudolph Klein who was the brother of a Major General Klaus Klein of the Swiss Defence Force. Now that name does ring a bell.'
Commandant Bourges looked through the files on his desk and seemed to find what he was looking for. Opening a file, he started to read the papers in it. 'Yes, this is interesting. It seems that some ten years ago Major General Klein was named as a possible German agent. There was no direct evidence and no action was taken against him. It is said that some of the information that he passed to the Germans came from diplomatic sources and there was some evidence to suggest that one of those sources was based in London. It begins to look as though it might have been Herr Schneider. Let me have a look at this file.'

He picked up another one and thumbed his way through it.

' This is a report prepared by the Swiss Security Service which looked at various Swiss embassies and consulates during the second world war. Yes, it says there were unconfirmed allegations that information from Britain was being passed to Switzerland and was then passed on to the Germans. So, it is possible that Herr Schneider was the person passing on information. He was the only non career diplomat at the embassy at that time. Of course, there is no proof that any information came from your lady.'
'No, but that chances do seem to be quite high. What about Herr Schneider, is anything known about him for the post war years?'
'It seems he returned to the family firm, retired and died a couple of years ago. The business was bought out by a German firm some twenty years ago.'
'Herr Schneider had a son, the one that Audrey Hope taught to speak English, and he was at her funeral. He gave his card to one of my colleagues. I think it might be worth speaking to him to see what he knows.'
'The Swiss are cautious people Chief Superintendent I doubt if he will tell you more than he thinks you need to know.'

Buxton took a taxi to the address on the card that Kurt Schneider had given to Inspector Thomasson. It was a very nice lakeside villa with immaculate gardens both on the road side and on the side that led down to the water. His knock on the door was answered by a man about fifty dressed in a light weight beige suit a pale-yellow shirt and a light green tie.

'Herr Schneider' Buxton said 'I am sorry to trouble you but as I happen to be in Zurich, I thought I would call. My name is Buxton and I am a police officer from England,' he produced his credentials and showed them to the man 'I am investigating the death of Miss Audrey Hope.'
'I knew Audrey had died but I had no idea it was a matter for the police.' The English was almost perfect.
'I am sorry to say that she was murdered.'
'Poor Audrey', he seemed generally upset. 'How can I help you? I knew her for almost the whole of my life but, in recent years our contact had been purely social. The exchange of Christmas cards and she would send me birthday greetings. If she came to Zurich we always met for a meal and a talk about old times. I can think of no-one who might wish her harm.'
'Your late father knew her as well I understand.'
'Yes, you could say he was the one who introduced us when he employed the young Audrey to teach me English. Their friendship lasted all of forty years, apart from the war years of course when Audrey could not come to this country.'
'But your father was in England for some of that time I believe ?'
'Yes, he was attached to the embassy.'
'And Miss Hope was also in London so I suppose they must have met.'
'I have no idea. I do not remember them speaking of doing so. London is of course a big place and there must have been a great many people there during those years. I would think it most unlikely their paths crossed.'
'Do you know what Miss Hope was doing at that time?'
'She simply said that she worked as a secretary in government office as I recall
.'
'Can you think, Herr Schneider, of anyone who might wish Miss Hope harm ?'
'Most assuredly not. She was a very nice lady.'
'I am sorry to have bothered you Herr Schneider and am grateful to you for your assistance.'

As he returned to his hotel Buxton smiled to himself. Commandant Bourges had been right. Either Kurt Schneider did not know anything or he was saying nothing. To settle the Swiss connection, he needed to know what exactly Audrey Hope did during the war.

That evening as he sat on the terrace of his hotel for dinner and looked out over the lake, he could not but think how much Doreen would have loved to be there with him and he with her.

 Fortunately, he had a friend who held a senior position in the Special Branch. Once back in Sussex he contacted his friend and asked for assistance from Special Branch in searching for information about government personnel during the second world war. As he suspected there were many thousand of these who had been processed by Special Branch. At the start of the war a great many people had been recruited on the old boy network. Either they had been to the right school or were the son or daughter of an acceptable chap. Later a more professional approach to screening was adopted. What he wanted to know was whether the name Audrey Hope was included in that list and, if so, where was she posted and what work had she done. As it was an official request for help his friend could not dismiss it out of hand however it would take some time to try and find the answer.
When the answer came it was sufficient to allow Buxton to widen his search. This led him to both MI5 and SIS. It became clear that theoretically at least she had possession of information which might have been of use to the enemy. This raised a supplementary question. Had there ever been evidence of a leak of information in any of the areas in which Audrey Hope had worked? Whilst there was no direct evidence indicating she had been involved there was a certain area where it was felt that sensitive information was reaching the Germans in time for them to cause operational problems to the allies.

For the first time there seemed to be a potential motive but why anyone should wait forty years to seek revenge was a puzzle to which he had no answer.

CHAPTER 28

Having spent the morning catching up with routine work and in updating the ACC on his trip to Switzerland Buxton settled down to consider how the information that had been gathered about Audrey Hope could lead to identifying her killer. Fortunately, he had a friend who held a senior position in the Special Branch. Now he was back in Sussex he contacted this friend and asked for assistance from Special Branch in searching for information about government personnel during the second world war. As he suspected there were many thousands who had been processed by Special Branch. At the start of the war a great many people had been recruited on the old boy network. Either they had been to the right school or were the son or daughter of an acceptable chap. Later a more professional approach to screening was adopted. What he wanted to know was whether the name Audrey Hope was included in that list and, if so, where was she posted and what work had she done. As it was an official request for help his friend could not dismiss it out of hand however it would take some time to try and find the answer.
When it came the answer came sufficient to allow Buxton to widen his search. This led him to both MI5 and SIS and it became clear that, theoretically at least, she had been in possession of information which might have been of use to the enemy. This raised a supplementary question. Had there ever been evidence of a leak of information in any of the areas in which Audrey Hope had worked? Whilst there was no direct evidence indicating she had been involved there was a certain area where it was felt that sensitive information was reaching the Germans in time for them to cause operational problems to the allies. Not only that but it seems that she had been a member of a body called the ANGLO-German Co-Operation Organisation in the thirties. This group was known to be pro-Nazi and had been closed down in 1940.

For the first time there seemed to be a potential motive but why anyone should wait forty years to seek revenge was a puzzle to which he had no answer.

If the motive had been what she had done during the war years then it seemed most likely that someone from that era had either been waiting for an opportune moment to take revenge or that it was only recently that they had obtained information about what they believed to be her role in passing information to the enemy. Added to this was the question as to why the location for the murder had been chosen. It could be that it was because it was somewhere where she could risk being seen. She was a member of the FG2 and at their function that would raise no questions. Also, someone has reported seeing a car parked off the road on the far side of the camp site. All he could say was it was a dark colour.

Yet another question was if the killer of Audrey Hope could be identified how, if at all, could they be linked to the death of Nigel Burgess? Had they been wrong all this time in thinking that there was just one killer? He felt sure that there must be a pointer in the enormous amount of evidence they had gathered on the two crimes.

There was one additional area that needed to be looked at. He gave MI5 and SIS a list of names of people who had surfaced during the investigations. Did any of them also appear in the records? Once again this was going to take time to find the answer.

In the meantime, he decided to carry out a thorough review of that evidence collected to try and see if they had missed anything important. To do this he summoned Inspector Thomasson and Sergeant Sparrow to a meeting. He did not ask Inspector Love as he was heavily engaged in the case of a bank cash machine being stolen by using a mechanical digger to pull it out of the wall in which it had been fitted.

'What I want to do 'Buxton told the two men 'is go through the files of evidence that we have accumulated to see if there is anything there that we seem to have missed.' He pointed at the piles of files on the table of the room where they were meeting. 'So, let's get started.'

To get a fresh mind on each file it was passed to the person who had not been involved with that part of the investigation because nothing is easier than to read what you think you should be seeing rather than what is actually being said.

CHAPTER 29

'Hello Donald, please come in'
Donald Craigton entered the house and went into the side room.
' What can I do to help? 'asked Megan Legg.
'I would like you to answer a question please Megan.'
'What question is that ?'
'Why did you kill Nigel Burgess and Audrey Hope?'
For a moment or two there was no reply and then Megan Legg said;
'How did you find out ?'
'It was like a jigsaw puzzle. I found one piece of information here and another
somewhere else until a complete picture began to appear.' You don't deny that
it was you?'
'Why should I ? '
'You must have had a reason for doing these terrible things.'
'I did. I had excellent reasons but I doubt if you would understand them.'
'I think I know why you killed Audrey Hope.'
'She was a traitor to her country who sent innocent men and women to a terrible
death. For that she deserved to be punished.'
'Isn't that what our system of justice is designed to do?'
'For our much-vaunted system of justice to work there is a need for evidence.
That evidence is sometimes insufficient to allow justice to be obtained even if
there can be little or doubt that guilt exists.'
'Proof is a necessary part of our justice. If you do without that then innocent
people are going to suffer for things they never did.'
'Some crimes are so abhorrent that the normal rules cannot apply.'
'But that does not give any of us the right to act as judge, jury and executioner.'
'An eye for an eye and a tooth for a tooth we are told.'
'We are also told that when asked how many times should we forgive, is it
seven the answer is no it is seventy times seven.'
'I suppose it's not reasonable to expect you to understand' Megan sat opposite
Donald and looked over his shoulder and out of the window.' To do that you
would have had to live through the things I lived through. You may not approve
but will you at least let me explain? '
'I wish you would because at the moment I am finding it impossible to
understand your motives.'
'To begin we have to go back to 1940. This country was under the greatest
threat it had ever been. The Nazis were just across the Channel and North Sea.
We were unbelievably weak and ill prepared. However, one man was
determined that we would not go down without a fight. Winston Churchill
ordered that; in the event of a German invasion a secret resistance should be set
up to cause as much havoc as possible behind their lines. Small groups of men

who knew their locality like the back of their hands were to be formed. No-one, apart from the members themselves and the organiser were to know who they were. If the Germans landed the first thing the members of a group were to do was to kill the one man who knew all their names. Then they were to go into hiding in one of the specially prepared secret hideouts that had been constructed and concealed in their area. From there they would emerge at night and commit acts of sabotage such as blowing up railway lines or bridges or killing senior German officers and then disappear into the night and back into their hideouts. It was reckoned that the life expectancy of such a group was just two weeks. Fortunately, the Germans never did come and the groups were disbanded. For the groups to operate successfully there had to be communications between them and their headquarters. Sometimes there were wireless sets hidden in the most unlikely places, for example under church altars or in priest holes in country houses. Messages had to get out from the groups and back to them. For this people were recruited to be messengers. People who knew the countryside and knew how to move about undetected. Women were not allowed to be part of the groups but they could and did act as messengers. They picked up messages from the most unlikely places. For example, hidden behind notices attached to telegraph poles, or from bottles on a rubbish dump or behind the frame that used to contain a bus timetable. These messages were then taken to the concealed radio centre which might be in the cellar of a disused cottage or a completely buried pill box. The messages were sent into the receiving centre by dropping them down a drainpipe or in a hollow space behind some bricks. There was a group of resisters in this village though I think that most of them have died by now. I was recruited as a messenger and rode round the countryside on my horse or my bike to pick up and deliver messages. I was younger, slimmer and much fitter in those days' she added with a laugh.
'I had heard that you were involved in that activity' Donald said.
'Why should you. We all signed the Official Secrets Act and my generation has by a large kept its word. When the units were disbanded the men, or most of them, were drafted into the forces. I was asked to go for an appointment in London. I am not sure if you know that I was educated for several years at a French convent school and spoke fluent French in those days. To cut a long story short I found myself attached to the SOE and was sent for training with a view to being dropped into occupied France as radio operator working with the French Resistance. Unfortunately, on my last training parachute drop I fell awkwardly and badly injured my left ankle. To this day it is held together by a metal plate and is why I can never wear high heeled shoes. Declared unfit for active service I was used to test those about to be dropped to make sure they knew their cover story and could tell it with convincing detail. It was during this work I met a man and fell in love. He was dropped into eastern France and was caught within two days. He was shot two days later as a spy. It was apparent that there had been a leak somewhere and we thought it was on the

French side where security was sometimes less than perfect. I was demobbed in early 1945 when the allies had recaptured the greater part of France. I came back to the village and kept house for my parents and then for my brother. I never met anyone else I wanted to marry. At the same time, I never forgot him or what had happened to him. One of my civilian interests was the Girl Guides and I was a Brownie or Guide Leader here in the village for thirty years. After I retired, I joined the FG2. One year Audrey Hope who was also a member of FG2 organised a visit to Switzerland and, as I had never visited that country, I joined the group. While we were there Audrey introduced us to a Swiss friend whom she had known for years. His name was Herr Dr Schneider. One day we were all went to a lake. Some sat and read, others went for a walk. I moved along the lakeside and found a quiet spot in the shade. Two people came along and sat down the other side of a bush where I had parked myself. They must have been unaware that I was there and had no idea I could hear what they said. They were talking German and it so happened I had learned that language at my convent school. What I heard was a bolt from the blue.'
'Did you recognise who was talking?' asked Donald.
'I certainly did. It was the Herr Dr Schneider and Audrey Hope. He said that a potential problem was on the horizon. It seemed that some German and American historians were starting to ask questions about the extent to which Switzerland or its citizens had aided the Axis during the war. It started, he said, with the Swiss banks and efforts to find out how much Nazi gold they were holding. It had moved on from that, when they did not get anything from the banks, to asking about Swiss nationals. At least two army officers were said to be under suspicion. Is there any indication that they are looking elsewhere Audrey asked? He thought not but it was necessary for everyone to be very careful about what they said and to whom. Audrey then said that surely, they did not expect Swiss diplomats of passing information to the Axis powers. Dr Schneider replied that in the current climate no-one or nothing was completely secure. But you used diplomatic mail Audrey said they could never find out what was said in that. Dr Schneider agreed that this was their best defence. It was then that Audrey dropped her bomb. I really don't think that anyone ever had or even has the least idea that we were meeting in London. It was nearly forty years ago. You are probably right agreed Herr Schneider. After all, Audrey said, those Lyons Corner Houses were always packed so the risk of our being recognised must have been minimal, added to which we never met in the same one twice in a row. Who could have noticed what appeared to be two single diners both of whom had copies of The Times on the table and that each of them picked up the other's copy when the first of them left? The fact that my copy contained information useful to the Axis would never have been suspected. You passed on that information via diplomatic mail to your contact in Zurich who in turn passed it to German intelligence. That way we could stop the British helping the French resistance and leave more troops on the Eastern

Front to fight the Bolsheviks. The British agents were rounded up before they could do any damage. At this point' Megan said 'someone else in our group came along and spoke to Audrey and that brought an end to their conversation. I now knew that Audrey Hope was a German spy in world war two. Not only that but she was giving them information regarding our agents about to be dropped into France. This must have included their code names and their drop zones. She had killed the only man I ever loved, not only that but if I had not crocked my ankle, I might very well have been one of her victims.'
'You didn't have any real evidence 'Donald said 'only the unsupported words you had heard.'
'I realised that 'Megan replied curtly 'I also realised that British security would not welcome someone trying to prove there was an active German agent in this country when, for decades, they have said they were all rounded up and turned into double agents or were executed. All I could do was use some contacts from those days to see if I could prove that Audrey Hope was in a position to do what she claimed.'
'Did you do that?'
'Yes. I was able to find out that she worked for SOE as someone who co-ordinated among other things the records of people who were sent on active service. She had been in a position to do what she claimed.'
'You felt that this gave you the right of revenge? 'Donald asked.
'I knew that if I didn't do something no-one else would.'
'But why kill Nigel Burgess he could not have been involved in espionage he was far too young?'
'Burgess was, in a different way, as much a corrupter of life as any dictator. He had made a large amount of money. How he did so I don't know but I should be surprised if it was all made honestly. He came to this village and set about wrecking its way of life. Small villages like this are, in some ways, relics from the past. Change happens more slowly here than in big towns. We have a settled way of life that has built up over the years and which makes Upper Burford a pleasant and civilised place in which to live. From day one Burgess tried to disrupt that settled way of life. To start with it was just small things like trying to stop the church bells on a Sunday morning. The he tried to get his landscape garden done for nothing on the grounds his rich friends would pass business to the designer. He behaved as if he owned the place, expecting everyone to allow him to do exactly what he wanted. It was getting worse. He wanted to stage a pop festival on the village green and, if that was not bad enough, he had plans to buy Verney's Copse to turn it into a place for paint ball shooting and off the road vehicles. Just imagine what a noise and nuisance that would have caused. But the biggest thing was that Verney's Copse was where the secret hiding place for the 1940 village resistance group headquarters. It is a piece of the history not just of this village but of the country. To have it vandalised by the

likes of Burgess was an unforgivable insult. People had been prepared to die to protect the village. It should be left as a memorial to those dark days'

'But hardly a sufficient reason to kill him surely.

'These people have to be stopped before they do too much damage. Just think of what may have been saved if Adolf Hitler had been stopped in 1923. Besides there was another reason for me to act now.'

'What was that?'

'I have been diagnosed as having a brain tumour. When they told me that it was inoperable, I realised there was this one chance to stop Burgess and to make Audrey Hope pay for her crimes. Remember I had been trained as a secret agent and that included how to kill silently. I had, against all regulations, kept the special knife that was issued to us. I still had the ability to move quietly and surprise an intended victim. An arm round the neck and one blow with the knife in the right place and it was instantaneous death. Burgess was no problem. I entered through the trees at the back of his house, hid behind a big water butt. When he sat down, I slipped out and did the job and was gone inside a minute. I am a member of FG2 but said I would not go to the camp fire. I told people I had had a migraine that evening and was in my bedroom in the dark. In fact, I drove over to the camp site, parked off the road on the far side of the site and made my way to the chapel. I wore my FG2 sweatshirt so if anyone saw me, they would think I was at the camp fire. I had sent Audrey a note the day before which contained part of a postcard on which I wrote "Be in the chapel at 9.00 on Thursday and bring this with you. I will have the other half. I need to warn you" and I put the initials HS and added Corner House. She swallowed the bait whole. I crept out from the trees and she was dead before she knew what had happened. I found the card in her pocket put it in my own pocket and crept back to the car. Now you know how and why I did what I did. I shall be dead before they can arrest me.'

'What if I tell the police what you have told me ?'

'You won't do that Donald. You are a good man and will keep the secret of the confessional.'

At that moment there was the sound of a car stopping outside. Donald got to his feet and looked out of the window.

'It's a police car ' he said.

'Then they are too late '

Megan put her hand in her cardigan pocket and then to her mouth. She gave a croak, stiffened and fell to the floor. She had kept not only her dagger but the cyanide pill she had been given so that, in the event of capture, if things had got too bad there was a way out.

They had got that bad and she chose her way out.

CHAPTER 30

The inquest on Megan Legge ruled that she had taken her own life while the balance of her mind was disturbed. Her funeral took place in the village church and was conducted by the Rector. Although it was planned to be a quiet event, there were many people from the village and from Guiding and her other interests who attended.

After the service and committal Donald Craigton had spent some time at The Six Bells where light refreshments had been arranged by her brother. Buxton had attended the service but gone, by agreement, to Craigford's house where he had been admitted by Harold Whitehouse who had sung in the choir at the funeral.

'A very sad occasion Chief Superintendent 'he said handing Buxton a cup of tea. 'I did not know the lady well but when our paths crossed, she was always very pleasant.'

'I never met her' said Buxton.

'His lordship was more upset than he cared to show at what had happened '

'I can imagine it must have been a shock to him '

'Whenever local people refer to him, they always comment on what a good man he is, as I have every reason to know. In my book he is indeed a Good Samaritan.'

At this point the door opened and Donald Craigford entered.

'Hello Richard 'he said and sat down heavily in an armchair. Without a word Harold produced a cup of tea for him. 'Thank you, Harold. This is much better than cheap champagne.'

'Will there be anything else my lord?'

'I don't think so thank you.'

Harold withdrew discreetly.

'Well Richard 'said Donald 'Not exactly the ending either of us were expecting.'

'No. I am not sure if we would ever have got there but for your saying that things that happen in a village like this sometimes have deep roots. When I found out that Audrey Hope had quite probably been an enemy agent it set me wondering if there was anyone who might have known this. I used Special Branch to search back through old records and they came up with a whole list of names, one of which rang a bell. Her alibi for the night Audrey Hope was killed was without any verification. It was quite possible she had slipped out while her brother was at his dinner and have been home again when he returned. Even so I had no clue as to why she should have killed Burgess.'

'Nor had I,' said Craigton.

'I realise that you will not tell me what she said to you at your fateful meeting.'

'Not will not Richard, but cannot.'

'Then I may as well tell you that she left an envelope with her bank to be opened on her death. Inside it was a letter addressed to the police. In it she set out in detail not only how she had killed Burgess and Hope but, also, why she had done so. She did not want anyone being falsely accused of what she had done.'

'Although I can never condone what she did ' said Craigton, 'I have to admire her honesty.'

'Was it a realistic motive Donald'

'Is there ever a realistic motive for killing two people?'

'Do you think the balance of her mind was disturbed?

'Not so much by discovering Audrey Hope's betrayal but that fact that she caused the death of Megan' sweetheart and other innocent men and women. Also, of course, she knew that she too could have been one of her victims'

'But what about Burgess?'

'He was, in her mind, an evil that had to be stopped. The fact that she knew she was dying probably made the decision easier for her.'

'Do you think the locals will add two and two when they hear that the inquest on Burgess is closed without any further action? 'asked Buxton.

'I doubt it. The local view will be that Burgess was a rogue and someone he had crossed or double crossed took their revenge. As for Audrey Hope my guess the verdict will be that it was some passing thug which, again, will meet the local prejudice.'

'Even so, you worked out the solution without all the information we had. And don't say it was just luck.' grinned Buxton. 'You always were a good cop.'

'The village needs closure. In the end her actions spoke louder than any words. The facts were there and it was down to the police to solve the case. I am pleased that it did'

'One good thing out of all of this is that we have met up again.' said Richard

'That's true and I look forward to seeing you from time to time without having our conversation dominated by unsolved murders. I have moved on from all that. My new life is more than satisfying.'

'You know Donald, when I first met you again, I could not work out why you should have left the Met to become a curate in a small village. Whatever your reasons I am sure you made the right choice. You are where you should be'.